The man was taking Clint's gun belt to a narrow room guarded by more gunmen.

"Is anyone expecting trouble on this boat?" Clint asked.

The big man shook his head and crossed his arms. "This is all just a precaution. Just have a seat and play some cards. Leave the rest to us."

"Someone may have stowed away," Clint said. "And I don't think it was just so he could sit in on a game."

That caused all the gunmen to straighten up and take notice. Their hands drifted toward their pistols, making Clint feel practically naked since his gun wasn't even in his possession.

"We'll look into it," the big man said. "Anything else you want to tell us?"

"Just that he's dangerous and good with a knife."

"Thank you. Good luck with your game."

Clint walked toward Mia's table. Now he just needed to figure out why nobody had asked what the stowaway looked like or where he was headed.

One possibility was that the guards were overly confident that they could find anyone who didn't belong on the riverboat.

Another possibility was that they already knew about the man with the knife. Either way, Clint decided to keep what he'd seen under his hat until he was talking to someone he knew he could trust. On a riverboat full of poker players, someone like that might be a little hard to come by.

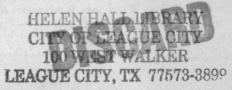

THE GUNSMITH

307

RED RIVER SHOWDOWN

J. R. ROBERTS

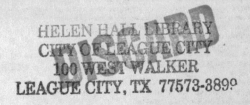

JOVE BOOKS, NEW YORK

THE BERKLEY PUBLISHING GROUP
Published by the Penguin Group
Penguin Group (USA) Inc.
375 Hudson Street, New York, New York 10014, USA
Penguin Group (Canada), 90 Eglinton Avenue East, Suite 700, Toronto, Ontario M4P 2Y3, Canada
(a division of Pearson Penguin Canada Inc.)
Penguin Books Ltd., 80 Strand, London WC2R 0RL, England
Penguin Group Ireland, 25 St. Stephen's Green, Dublin 2, Ireland (a division of Penguin Books Ltd.)
Penguin Group (Australia), 250 Camberwell Road, Camberwell, Victoria 3124, Australia
(a division of Pearson Australia Group Pty. Ltd.)
Penguin Books India Pvt. Ltd., 11 Community Centre, Panchsheel Park, New Delhi—110 017, India
Penguin Group (NZ), 67 Apollo Drive, Mairangi Bay, Auckland 1311, New Zealand
(a division of Pearson New Zealand Ltd.)
Penguin Books (South Africa) (Pty.) Ltd., 24 Sturdee Avenue, Rosebank, Johannesburg 2196,
South Africa

Penguin Books Ltd., Registered Offices: 80 Strand, London WC2R 0RL, England

This is a work of fiction. Names, characters, places, and incidents either are the product of the author's imagination or are used fictitiously, and any resemblance to actual persons, living or dead, business establishments, events, or locales is entirely coincidental.

RED RIVER SHOWDOWN
A Jove Book / published by arrangement with the author

PRINTING HISTORY
Jove edition / July 2007

ISBN: 978-0-515-14323-2

JOVE®
Jove Books are published by The Berkley Publishing Group,
a division of Penguin Group (USA) Inc.,
375 Hudson Street, New York, New York 10014.
JOVE is a registered trademark of Penguin Group (USA) Inc.
The "J" design is a trademark belonging to Penguin Group (USA) Inc.

PRINTED IN THE UNITED STATES OF AMERICA

10 9 8 7 6 5 4 3 2 1

ONE

Clint received the letter in an envelope sealed with wax. When Rick Hartman handed it to him, he did so with a raised pinky and an exaggerated flourish.

"A letter for you, sire," Rick said as he waved the envelope in front of Clint's face.

Clint was sitting at a small table in Hartman's saloon. Sometimes, Rick's Place felt like the closest thing Clint had to a home. And sometimes, that home came complete with a brother that seemed to thrive on getting under his skin.

"Are you going to hand that to me or dance around with it some more?" Clint asked.

"Go on and take it, my lord."

After making a slow reach for the envelope and having it pulled away at the last second, Clint snatched it from Rick's hand so quickly that the saloon owner didn't even realize right away that the envelope was gone. When he finally noticed his hand was empty, Rick chuckled and walked back around his bar.

It was the middle of the afternoon, and the West Texas heat was bad enough to keep even the serious gamblers away. That meant the saloon was practically empty except

1

for Rick, Clint and a few regulars that were too drunk to move.

"Who's it from?" Rick asked from across the room.

Clint was finishing up a plate of fried chicken and wiping his hands as he said, "If you'd give me a moment, I'll open it and see. Actually, I'm surprised you didn't already take a look for yourself."

"I almost did. It ain't too often that I get mail as fancy as that. What's that on the back?"

"Wax."

"I know that, smart ass," Rick replied. "What's that seal?"

After wiping his hands clean, Clint picked up the envelope and took a closer look. "Looks just like a fancy M."

"You recognize it?"

"No. Should I recognize it?"

Rick walked around the bar again and brought a beer along with him. He sat down across from Clint. "In the old days, them seals meant something. Sometimes, it was even a royal . . . uhh . . ."

"Crest," Clint said before Rick could swing in the breeze for too long. "You mean a royal crest."

Rick snapped his fingers and nodded. "That's right!" In a thick, almost theatrical drawl, he added, "Us Texas boys don't know too much about kings and such."

"And I do?" Clint asked.

"Well, what are you waiting for? Aren't you going to open it?"

"After all this buildup, I thought I should savor the moment."

Lifting his beer to his mouth, Rick grumbled, "Jesus, he gets one royal decree and he thinks he's something special."

Although Clint had been purposely dragging this on because he could practically feel Rick's curiosity boiling over, he couldn't get himself to wait much longer. Clint slipped one finger beneath the envelope's flap and pulled until the wax snapped free of the paper. Most of the ornate

M remained intact, leaving a red stain where it had once been stuck.

Clint removed the small, folded piece of paper inside the envelope and was careful to keep it hidden behind his own hand.

"Well?" Rick asked. "What is it?"

"Do you recall what curiosity did to the cat?"

"Yeah. The same thing I'm gonna do to you if you don't stop acting like a jackass."

Clint finally allowed himself to laugh as he dropped his hand and leaned back in his chair to read the card. The writing was as ornate as the seal and done in a much more flowing script than the lettering on the front of the envelope. It took a few seconds for Clint to adjust to the script after reading so many newspapers and hastily scribbled notes. Once his eyes got used to the elegant lettering, he nodded and looked back to Rick.

"It seems that I am cordially invited to the *Misty Morning*," Clint said.

Rick's brow furrowed and he asked, "The *Misty Morning*? What the hell is that?"

"A riverboat. It seems there's going to be some high-stakes games held on this boat to christen its first trip along the Red River."

"Good Lord Almighty," Rick said. "You mean to tell me all that fancy presentation was to announce a card game?"

"Not just a card game. There's going to be tournaments held from the minute the boat gets moving. According to this, there's going to be poker, roulette, dice, faro and just about anything else that a man can lose money on."

Shaking his head, Rick said, "Lose is right. That boat's probably got its own supply of cheats and cardsharps just as sure as it's got a supply of booze to keep the suckers' purse strings loose."

"Good thing I'm no sucker," Clint replied. "In fact, my luck's been running pretty good lately."

"That why you haven't played more'n a few hands of poker since you've been back in Labyrinth?"

Clint spread his arms to motion toward the rest of the nearly empty saloon. "It's kind of hard to play a few hands of anything when there isn't anyone around."

Rick was still shaking his head as he got to his feet and walked back to his bar. It seemed that he soon found the task of straightening the bottles more interesting than the letter in Clint's hand. "So it's been slow. You wanna gamble? There's plenty of places around here to do it. You want a poker tournament? I can throw one anytime you like."

Hearing that, one of the drunks at the bar lifted his head and asked, "There gonna be a poker tournament?"

Rick didn't even bother answering the drunk's question. All he had to do was wait another few seconds and the man's head drooped forward once more. "Sorry I wasted your time," Rick said to Clint. "If I'd known what was in that envelope, I wouldn't have made such a fuss."

After waiting a few seconds, Clint said, "You know, a man who owned a saloon could get a lot of business if more gamblers knew about his place." He fanned himself with the invitation and nodded as if he was simply talking to himself. "Gamblers on a boat like that might even drop enough money at a nice enough place to make the owner rich."

"What's your angle, Adams?" Rick asked sternly.

"If a certain saloon owner could put up half my stake, I might just talk his place up to make sure at least a few of them headed that way after the *Misty Morning* docked again. The Red River landing isn't too far of a ride from here, after all."

"You got the gambling itch, huh?"

"Things have been a bit slow for me, also. There aren't even enough prospects around to make it worth getting my old tools and wagon out of the livery right now. A healthy win or two would go a long way to keep my finances stable."

"And what about the finances of a potential partner who

doesn't have lots of money to risk staking a lousy gambler?" Rick asked.

Clint smirked and replied, "Staking a lousy gambler would be stupid."

Slowly, Rick started to nod. "You got a point. You also got yer partner. Hell, it'll be worth the money just to get you out of my place for a while."

TWO

The *Misty Morning* was supposed to be docked at a spot along the Red River that was fifty miles southeast of Amarillo. Clint covered the first twenty-five of those miles without seeing more than a few other riders along the way. Although he was in good spirits, Clint was carrying a hefty amount of Rick Hartman's money, so he greeted those other riders with a friendly tip of his hat and moved on.

After covering mile number thirty, Clint spotted another horse a little ways in front of him. The horse was moving at a steady pace and had kept its back to Eclipse the entire time. Without much else to look at, Clint watched that horse run in front of him the way he would watch the sun slowly set in a few hours.

The show got a little more interesting as three other riders approached from the south, split up and closed in on the first rider from three different angles. Clint recognized the way the other riders approached as though he could see the hungry look in their eyes. Reflexively, Clint snapped Eclipse's reins to get the Darley Arabian moving at something closer to running speed. He didn't know if those other three had spotted him yet, so Clint wasn't anxious to make noise or kick up dust to draw attention to himself.

Since the three riders weren't too concerned about keeping quiet, it wasn't long before the one who'd been there originally noticed the others closing in. That first rider twisted in the saddle and looked around to pick out each of the other three.

Clint spotted the glint of sunlight off of iron and knew that one of the three riders had drawn a gun. He touched his heels to Eclipse's sides and hung on as the stallion burst into a full gallop and thundered over the dry Texas soil.

By this time, the first rider had drawn a gun as well. In fact, that rider even got off the first shot. The sound was lost amid the pounding in Clint's ears, but he could see the smoke easily enough from where he was. Even though the modified Colt had been drawn from the holster at his hip, Clint kept from pulling his trigger until he got a little closer.

The gunfire cracked through the air like a Fourth of July celebration as all three riders opened fire and the first one answered right back. The four horses didn't seem to be rattled by the commotion, but they were moving fast enough to make it difficult for the riders to hit their targets. That didn't keep the three from firing again and again as the first one turned back around to pay closer attention to the trail ahead.

Clint felt like he'd been shot from a cannon. Eclipse covered the distance between him and the nearest of the three riders in no time at all. Even as he closed to within pistol range, Clint held off on firing until he got a better look at the man in front of him.

The rider wore a blue bandanna wrapped around the lower half of his face. As soon as he turned around to look at Clint with wide, surprised eyes, he aimed quickly and sent a bullet in Clint's direction.

It was Clint's impulse to duck low, but that wasn't necessary to dodge the incoming lead. The shot had been taken quickly and from the back of a running horse, which

meant it had little to no chance of hitting anything but open
air. Just to be safe, Clint pulled Eclipse's reins to the left
and steered between two of the three riders.

The next rider's face was also mostly covered by a bandanna. Now that Clint was close enough, he could see that
the third wore a bandanna as well. He was also close
enough to see that the slender shape in the first horse's saddle was much too attractive to belong to a man.

Having watched the first rider for several miles, Clint
had suspected it might be a woman. None of that came
from her riding style, however, since she handled her horse
better than most men. Her shoulders and waist were just a
little too narrow, which had made Clint wonder about her
ever since he'd first spotted that horse in front of him.

As much as Clint wanted to lend a hand, he realized that
he didn't even know who any of these people were. For all
he knew, those three men were a posse closing in on a
wanted murderer. The woman could just as well be in the
right, but there was no way for Clint to know for certain.

It did help sway his thinking when the closest of the
three masked riders looked to the other two and shouted,
"Shoot this son of a bitch!"

THREE

Suddenly, lead filled the air around Clint's head. Shots blazed all around him and drew closer with every pull of the trigger. Clint fired back as well, but he was too busy steering Eclipse and hanging onto the stallion's neck to take very careful aim.

Rather than waste ammunition with wild shooting, Clint pulled on Eclipse's reins and sent the Darley Arabian into a sharp turn that pointed his nose directly at one of the masked riders. Any other animal might have fought the command or simply ignored it, but Eclipse kept his faith in Clint and charged.

Fortunately, Eclipse was fast enough to put a scare into the other horse as he rushed toward it. The other horse didn't rear, but it turned in the opposite direction its masked rider had wanted to go. The masked man went from agitated to downright panicked when a few shots aimed at Clint hissed dangerously close to his own head.

"Ease up, god dammit!" the masked rider shouted as Clint passed alongside of him. Before he could say or do anything else, the rider felt Clint's elbow catch him square in the chest. The blow didn't do much damage, but it knocked the rider over the side of his horse, where he dangled less than an inch from the ground thanks to one stubborn foot caught in a stirrup.

Clint steered in another direction as he tried to think of a way to get everyone stopped so he could decide if he'd just made a big mistake. The masked men were thinking along those same lines, but took less time to decide on a course of action.

After a few hand signals passed between the two masked men still in their saddles, both of them turned their guns on the woman and opened fire. She did a fine job of clinging to her horse and giving the men a smaller target, but there was nowhere for the horse to hide.

Bullets slapped into the animal's flesh, tore through muscle and bone and then brought the horse screaming to its knees.

Clint gritted his teeth at the sight of the animal dropping to the ground. Despite the wounds it had been given, the horse still fought to remain upright, as if to give its rider as big a chance as possible to jump clear. She did exactly that and landed in a ball well away from the fallen horse.

Her landing knocked the wind from her lungs and rattled her pretty badly, but she still managed to get to her feet. She hadn't been able to hold onto her gun and started running the moment she realized that both of her hands were now empty. By the time she looked up from those hands, the woman was being picked off her feet and swept away.

"Good Lord!" she shouted as she instinctively grabbed onto the arm that was wrapped around her waist.

Clint held onto her and swung her onto the saddle in front of him. It was a little awkward steering Eclipse that way, but all he needed to do was bring the stallion to a halt. "Just a moment," Clint said as he straightened his arm and sighted along the barrel of his Colt. "We'll get this cleared up soon."

After saying that, Clint squeezed his trigger and sent a

round toward the head of the closest masked man's horse. Unlike the shots that had brought the woman's animal down, Clint's bullet was perfectly aimed and not fatal. It buzzed past the horse's head so closely, that it burned away the last of the animal's composure.

Just as the masked man was about to fire, his horse reared up and nearly threw him off its back.

The third masked man saw Clint aiming his Colt at him next. Rather than try his own luck where the other two had failed, he lowered his gun and pulled back on his reins.

"This ain't none of your business, mister," the third man said from behind his bandanna.

"That's why I thought we could take a breath before anyone got killed."

The horse with the man dangling from its stirrup had slowed to a halt and now moved in a slow circle as its rider struggled to pull himself free. When he finally did get his foot loose, he dropped onto his back with a pained grunt.

The second rider's horse was still fussing and resisting the reins, leaving the third to do most of the talking.

As soon as Eclipse came to a stop, the woman jumped down and ran toward her own fallen animal. By the time she got to its side, it was barely moving.

Clint saw two of the riders eyeing her as if she was the last piece of steak on an otherwise empty plate. Feeling those men's anxiousness as if it was a wave of heat in the air, he positioned himself between them and her. "What's going on here?" he asked. "Why'd you open fire on her?"

None of the men were answering, although they were all now back in their saddles.

"Explain how I've overstepped my bounds and I'll be glad to leave," Clint told the masked men.

The three men didn't speak with words. Instead, they swapped a few quick glances and then acted as one.

Lifting their arms, two of them aimed at the woman while one aimed at Clint.

Clint's reaction was quick and instinctual as he picked out one target and fired. His bullet went right where he'd wanted it to go and drilled a messy hole through one rider's shoulder. His second shot was intended to knock another rider from his saddle, but missed since that man was already on the move.

Clint's finger was relaxed upon his trigger as the third rider prepared to fire another shot. Just then, a gunshot blasted from Clint's right. He turned to find the woman standing beside her horse with a smoking pistol in her hands.

Her bullet caught the third rider in the chest.

The other two masked men rode away as if their tails were on fire.

FOUR

Clint could have chased those two men down.

With Eclipse warmed up and raring to go, Clint knew he wouldn't have had any trouble catching up to those men and running a few circles around them before figuring out what to do next. But even a fleeting glimpse of those men's eyes told Clint all he needed to know. They meant to get the hell away from there, and they would do anything to cover themselves along the way.

A cornered animal was never something to fool with, so Clint let them go and shifted his attention back to the ones who were left behind.

When he'd heard the shot, his hand immediately brought up the Colt. Clint lowered the pistol back into its holster when he saw the woman standing over her horse.

She still held her own gun in hand as she looked into the animal's eyes before they glazed over. "God damm it," she said as tears rolled down her cheek.

"You didn't have a choice," Clint told her. Reaching out with one hand, he pushed her hand down so she was no longer pointing the gun at the wounded horse's head.

When she turned her eyes to him, the fire in them was

unmistakable. "I know I didn't have a choice," she snapped. "Thanks to those cowardly assholes."

"Who were they?" Clint asked. "Then again, you could also tell me who you are. Start with either one, but be quick about it."

"Why? Are you going to try and rob me, too?"

"Actually, I'm still not sure if I let the wrong ones go."

The fire in the woman's eyes flared up a bit, but then quickly died away. She looked at her own hand as if she'd forgotten about the gun she was holding. "Sorry about that," she told him in a softer voice. "After I found this pistol, I should have helped you follow them. I just couldn't bear to see Harriet in so much pain."

"I'm not talking about that. I'd like to know how things could go to hell so damn fast. I've had you in my sight for miles and those men rode up on you from out of nowhere."

"You were following me?" she asked.

Clint shook his head as he walked over to the body of the rider who'd been shot in the chest. Just to make sure, he checked the man's shirt and vest. There wasn't a badge pinned anywhere, so that put his mind a bit more at ease.

"I wasn't exactly following you," he told her. "Just heading the same direction."

She nodded and looked down at the dead man. Seeing those vacant eyes staring up toward the sky seemed to hit her at that moment. Suddenly, she barely seemed able to stand up. Her gun slipped from her fingers and she pressed both hands to her face. "Good Lord," she said through her fingers. "Is he . . . ?"

"As a doornail," Clint replied.

"Oh God. Those others were going to kill me, too. They were shooting at me. Shooting at both of us."

"You're just now realizing this?"

"It's not exactly every day that men like this shoot at me." Her eyes remained fixed upon Clint as she walked toward him. "You saved my life."

"Actually, things seemed to get bad right about when I rode in."

"No," she said while shaking her head. "You saved my life. They were going to kill me. They've been following me ever since I left Amarillo."

"Do you have any notion of why they'd be after you?" Clint asked.

She nodded and walked over to where her horse was lying. Kneeling down, she reached beneath the saddle and struggled to open the flap of the saddlebag that was pinned between the horse and the ground. She held a small leather pouch, but the pouch had been pulled halfway open as she'd taken it from the crushed bag.

At first, Clint thought he was mistaken. Then again, it would have been pretty difficult to confuse a thick stack of money for anything else. "Damn," Clint said. "How much is that?"

"Twenty-five thousand," she replied. "Those men knew I had it on me and they knew I'd be riding alone with it."

Clint glanced from the woman to the trail that had just been used by the surviving attackers. Neither sight brought him a bit of comfort. "If those men know about that money, we should get the hell out of here."

"You think there's more of them?"

"I think they'll be awfully quick to get more of whatever they need to get their hands on that kind of cash. Take whatever you need and come with me."

The first thing she did was walk back to the horse and dig around in the same saddlebag.

"Actually," Clint said, "just come along with me now. We may not have enough time to collect all of your things."

She kept digging around, but pulled her hands free before Clint could become too anxious. In her grasp, there was another stack of bills. This one was slightly smaller than the first one, but was still impressive. "This is the rest of what they were probably after," she said.

"Is there any more in there?" Clint asked.

"No." After stuffing the money into the pockets of her denim jacket, she unbuckled the saddlebag on the top side of the horse and handed it to Clint. "This is most of my clothes. If I need anything else, I can always get it later."

"Where are you headed?"

"The *Misty Morning*," she replied. "It's a boat docked along the—"

"Yeah," Clint interrupted. "I know where it's docked."

FIVE

Her name was Mia Hayley. They didn't introduce themselves to each other until after they'd put the spot of the
ambush well behind them. Even for a while after that, Mia
sat behind Clint with her head resting on his shoulder as if
she'd fallen asleep. Just to stay on the safe side, Clint kept
his Colt strapped into its holster and kept one hand resting
upon the grip at all times.

Once the scenery around them changed, so did the feeling between Clint and Mia. The land on either side of the
trail was getting greener by the minute, and the smell of the
river grew thicker in the air. Mia introduced herself in a
chipper voice. Clint thought she might have gotten some
sleep after all.

"How did you hear about the *Misty Morning*?" she
asked.

"I got an invitation."

"Was it like this one?"

Clint felt her hand brush over his shoulder and turned to
see the same fancy lettering on a similar piece of paper.
Even though he could see the similarities right away, Clint
took the invitation and read it over. His eyes spent most of

their time lingering over the spot where the address was inscribed.

"That's the one," he said while handing it back to her.

"Do you know who's running this whole thing?"

"No."

"Aren't you curious as to how you got invited?" she asked.

Clint shifted so he could look over his shoulder and found Mia grinning mischievously back at him. She was a slender woman with a strong grip. Even though her arms were fairly skinny, they held onto him as though a hurricane wasn't about to shake her loose. Her face was thin as well, with high cheekbones, a pert nose and lips shaped like a small bow. Black hair hung to her shoulders and was held back by a simple strip of leather.

"You seem pretty anxious to tell me, so why don't you start with your ideas," Clint said.

"I'll bet a gambler got tired of riding the circuit, so he arranged to have all the players brought to him. He may have even set up a few crooked games to make sure he came out ahead."

"I was expecting something more sinister, considering how we met up."

"You mean those men who attacked me?"

Clint could feel her shrug as she cinched her arms around his waist a bit more.

"They had their eye on me at the bank," she replied. "They followed me out of Amarillo and I thought I'd lost them along the way. I guess I didn't." After a few seconds, she perked up again and asked, "What about you? What's your theory on the mysterious invitation?"

"Actually, I'd say yours sounds pretty good. It's definitely not as exciting as mine."

"Let's hear it."

"I play a lot of cards wherever I go," Clint explained. "Gamblers keep track of every little detail where the games and players are concerned, so I thought someone kept me in mind for something like this. Besides, I usually get roped into something else while I'm at things like these."

Mia laughed. "Something like guarding the money or chasing down the cheats, I'd guess."

"Usually something like that."

"Are you a lawman?"

Clint looked farther up the trail, silently hoping to see the riverboat so he could point Mia's curiosity in another direction. Since there wasn't anything particularly interesting in sight, Clint replied, "Not exactly."

"You sure acted like a lawman."

"A lawman wouldn't have charged headfirst into that much lead like I did."

"No," she said as she squeezed him a bit tighter. "He wouldn't."

"Well, don't be too impressed," Clint said. "I just hope my luck holds as well as it did when those men were shooting at us."

"Luck is only important for folks who don't know what they're doing. I'll bet you don't need one bit of luck . . ." Mia's hand drifted over Clint's stomach and quickly brushed along the inside of his thigh. "No matter what you do."

SIX

The riverboat came into view at the same time as the rest of the dock. Clint rode over the top of a hill, looked down and saw it all spread in front of him like a painting. Next to the dock itself, there was a strip of small buildings with people moving among them like busy ants.

"Is that the *Misty Morning*?" Mia asked.

Looking at the riverboat, Clint shrugged and replied, "I hope so. There aren't any other boats docked nearby."

"What about the rest of it? Are those all shipping offices? Do you think I could buy some nicer clothes? I had to leave some of my dresses behind."

Instead of trying to answer Mia's excited questions, Clint snapped his reins and told her to hang on. Eclipse started running as if he was just as anxious to get a closer look at the dock. Before Mia could catch her breath long enough to ask any more questions, they were close enough to start reading the signs painted over the buildings near the dock. Clint steered toward the clothing store before Mia even had a chance to ask about it.

The buildings alongside the dock looked like a section of street had been plucked out of a good-sized town and dropped in its current spot. There was one of just about anything a man could want, ranging from a saloon to a furniture shop. But Clint wasn't interested in getting first crack at merchandise that had been loaded off a boat. Instead, he went to the shipping office in the middle of the street.

"Excuse me," Clint asked the tall man behind the counter.

The man stooped down with his elbows resting on the counter. His skinny nose looked like it had been stolen from a snowman's face, and his clothes looked as if they'd been donated by a scarecrow. When he spoke, it was in a low, rumbling grunt. "Can I help you?"

"Is that the *Misty Morning* out there?"

"Can't you see for yourself?"

Clint waited for a few seconds, until it became clear that the man wasn't going to say anything else. Letting out a sigh, Clint turned to look out the window where the riverboat could be seen. Actually, Clint had to step to another spot since the riverboat was so close that he couldn't see the name of it right away.

"That one says *Red River Runner*," Clint said.

The clerk had already gotten back to whatever he'd been doing before. Shrugging, he grunted, "There you go."

"Isn't the *Misty Morning* supposed to be docking here?"

"Were you supposed to meet it here?"

"Yes," Clint said.

"There you go."

Tensing his fist for a moment and then forcing himself to let it go, Clint said, "I rode all the way from Labyrinth to get here. I'm tired. I'm hungry. I'm also about one second away from reaching over this counter, dragging you over it and tossing you out that window."

Hearing that, the clerk snapped his head back up as if he'd only just noticed Clint was standing there.

Clint smiled at him and said, "There you go."

The clerk sputtered a few times to himself and turned

around to the wall behind him. There were several boards hanging from nails on that wall, and each of those boards had papers attached to it by twine. After picking out one of the boards, the clerk flipped through the papers and tapped it with his finger. "The *Misty Morning*'s supposed to be here, but it got delayed."

"For how long?"

"I just got word about it over the wire and it didn't mention how long. It just said it was going to be delayed. Usually, if a boat's going to be more than a few hours late, they mention it. Otherwise, they just pass on word that they're gonna be . . ."

"Delayed?" Clint asked.

The clerk nodded.

"That wasn't so hard, now was it?"

The clerk shook his head.

"Is there a way for me to be notified when the *Misty Morning* gets here?"

"Sure," the clerk said as he straightened up and made his way to his original spot. "Are you going to be staying around here?"

"Is there a place to stay nearby?"

"There's the Boathouse just down the way and there's some rooms for rent in the saloon."

"The Boathouse it is," Clint said.

"I can have someone run over there to let you know as soon as we get word on when your boat's due in."

"That's very helpful of you." Clint reached into his pocket, which caused the clerk to twitch. When he lifted his hand again, Clint held out a silver dollar and set it on the counter. "That's for your trouble. Sorry if I was a little short with you before."

The clerk reached for the dollar the way a varmint might reach for a bit of cheese in the middle of a snare. When he picked it up without incident, he tucked it away and showed Clint a nervous grin. "No problem, sir. Happens all the time."

On his way out of the office, Clint muttered, "I wonder why that is."

After stepping onto the well-maintained boardwalk connecting the long row of buildings, Clint looked down to the clothing shop where he'd last seen Mia. She was nowhere to be found, and judging by the look that had been on her face when they'd arrived, she wouldn't be seen for some time.

The Boathouse was easy enough to spot since it was a three-floor building at the other end of the row. Clint noticed a livery a little farther down and took Eclipse's reins to see about accommodations for the Darley Arabian.

Several folks wandered up and down the row. Most of them were stepping in and out of the shops or peeking into the windows. A few of them looked like sailors, and they guided Clint's eyes directly to the saloon the clerk had mentioned. Two other men didn't seem interested in the shops or the saloon, however.

When he first spotted them, Clint tipped his hat and led Eclipse down the street. As he'd glanced over to the river-boat docked to his left, Clint turned a bit more and found that the two men had decided to walk behind him. Since he was already looking in that direction, Clint turned and took another quick glance at them.

The men were dressed in plain, dark suits with jackets worn open to expose a few spare bullets looped into their gun belts. Although they didn't acknowledge Clint's glance, they didn't look away either. Clint turned away from them and kept walking to the livery. By the time he got there, he was feeling downright foolish for being so suspicious of a few men walking down the street. If there had been more than one street, Clint might have been more concerned.

The livery was set up to keep horses comfortable for extended amounts of time, and Clint didn't mind paying a bit extra on Eclipse's behalf. When he stepped out of the livery, those men in the dark suits were nowhere to be found.

SEVEN

The sun was halfway down, which cast a shimmering orange glow over the Red River. Some of the water lapping against the paddle wheel of the departing *Red River Runner* turned the light into a brighter yellow. Clint watched the riverboat pull away, admiring the way the sunlit water actually made the paddle wheel appear to be on fire.

Some of the happier folks on the deck of the boat waved to the folks on shore. Clint waved back and lifted his drink to a kid who looked happy enough to bust out of his skin. When the kid found someone else to wave at, Clint lowered his drink and took a sip.

He was sitting in front of the Boathouse on a porch swing hanging from the awning. Stretching one arm along the back of the swing, Clint glanced toward the end of the street where Mia had gone when they'd first gotten there. Unlike all the other times he'd looked that way, she was actually there.

"I was beginning to wonder about you," Clint said once she was close enough to hear.

Mia slowed down to come to a stop a few feet from the swing. Holding her arms out, she twirled in a quick circle and said, "I had to wait for my new dresses to be altered. What do you think?"

24

Mia's dress was made out of dark brown velvet and was held in place with thin, black ribbons laced down the middle. Her skirt had a few bits of fringe toward the bottom, but wasn't gussied up in any way. Even so, Clint wasn't quick to take his eyes off of her.

Although the dress was nice, he was more interested in the way the material clung to her body. The velvet flowed over her slender hips and pert breasts as if it had been smeared onto her body. Mia's curves were slight, but suited her perfectly.

Catching himself before too much time had slipped by, Clint said, "It's pretty."

Mia smiled as if she knew exactly why it had taken Clint so long to answer and sat down on the swing beside him. "This is nice. There's another one that's pretty. The other ones are beautiful."

"I hope I'll get a chance to see them."

"You're still going on the boat, aren't you?" she asked.

"If it ever gets here."

Mia waved Clint off and leaned back. "It's going to get here. It'll just be a little late, is all."

"How do you know that?" Clint asked. "Did you sneak out of that shop for a few minutes when I wasn't looking?"

"No. This isn't exactly a town, you know. It's a port. Everyone knows every boat that's due to float by here. My seamstress told me not to expect the *Misty Morning* until . . . well . . . morning."

"Damn."

"What's the matter?"

"I thought I'd be on the boat sipping a drink by now."

Mia scooted in a little closer to him and said, "This isn't so bad. I'm sure there'll be plenty of cards to be played when the boat gets here."

"Yeah. You're probably right."

"Probably? You think those gamblers will get bored of poker by the time you step foot onto the deck?"

"No," Clint said. "I'm just starting to think this might not be such a good idea. With you being the one who was attacked and everything, I would have thought you'd be thinking the same thing."

"Hardly," Mia said cheerily. "I think the worst has already happened. What better time than that to start gambling? After being shot at, losing a few dollars doesn't seem so bad."

Clint's arm slipped off the edge of the swing and landed on Mia's shoulders. Rather than lift his arm, he settled it around her and gave her a quick squeeze. She nestled against him as if she'd been waiting all day for that exact move to be made.

"You've got a point there," he said.

"Good. Now buy me a drink."

"Starting early, huh?"

"Sure," Mia said. "What are you having?"

"Lemonade."

"And I thought all gunfighters drank nothing but whiskey."

"Then go get yourself a whiskey," Clint said. "You hit more than I did when we first crossed paths."

Suddenly, Mia's smile dropped away. It was gone so quick that Clint felt as if it had been knocked off her face. He felt horrible when he realized that he'd been the one to make that smile disappear.

Clint shifted so he was sitting sideways on the swing. That way, he could look directly in her eyes when he told her, "I'm sorry about that. It just slipped."

She shrugged and nodded, but wouldn't look back at him.

Placing one finger under her chin, Clint lifted her head a bit and then rubbed the backs of his fingers along her smooth cheek. "I'm really sorry. That was a mean thing to say."

"Do you think I'm a killer?" she asked quietly.

"Not at all. Those men came after you. I saw them.

They shot first. They might not have hit you right away, but they would have gotten to it sooner or later."

"I just want to forget about it."

"You can't do that, Mia," Clint told her. "You had every right to defend yourself, and you shouldn't feel bad about what you did. You can't just forget about it, though. You try to do that and you'll only be haunted by it later."

"So . . . what do I do?"

"Face it down right now and make peace with it. Those assholes wanted to kill you and you stopped them. End of story. Once you do that, the whole mess will just fade on its own. At least," Clint added, "until another asshole like me dredges it up."

Mia straightened her back and turned so her shoulders were squared to his. "I'm facing you down and making peace with you," she declared. Soon, her smile came back again. "Now buy me that drink."

EIGHT

Clint bought Mia her drink.

He also bought the next round of drinks.

She insisted on buying the next round.

After that, things got a little hazy.

It didn't take long for them to notice that they weren't the only gamblers waiting for the *Misty Morning*. Not only was the saloon the only building in the port that was full and noisy after midnight, but there were poker games being played on nearly every flat surface in the room. That included the bar, which hosted a game for four people who leaned on their elbows to try and keep their cards out of sight.

There was no stage in the saloon, but a man eventually sat in a corner and started to sing. He was quickly surrounded by a few sailors who drowned him out when they started singing along.

Mia wandered into a card game for a few hands, lost every one of them and wandered away. When she stumbled back to Clint's table, he was just drunk enough to laugh at her.

"That was pathetic," he chided. "You should just hand

28

over all your money now and save yourself the humiliation when the boat arrives."

Leaning over a bit too far, Mia put one hand next to her mouth as if that would help once she shouted to be heard over the raucous singing. "I let them win," she slurred. "They'll be easy to bluff once we get on the boat."

"Great strategy," Clint replied. After taking a drink of his beer, he asked, "How much did it cost you?"

"A hundred dollars. Maybe two." Mia actually seemed proud of herself for a while. Once that wore off, she scowled and asked, "You think that was too much?"

"It was worth it to teach those stinking gamblers a lesson."

Clint managed to hold on for a second or two before he busted out laughing. Even though she laughed a bit herself, Mia still swatted Clint on the shoulder.

"You wait and see," she told him. "I'll win plenty more than you."

Clint nodded and made sure he was out of her reach. "Oh, I'm sure you will."

"I'm not joking."

"I know. You're drunk as hell, but you're not joking."

Mia got up, pushed Clint into his chair and then sat in his lap. Draping one arm around the back of his neck, she used her other hand to poke Clint in the chest as she asked, "You don't believe me, do you?"

"I'm sure you'll win plenty, Mia."

"Don't talk to me like that."

"Like what?"

"Like you don't believe me!"

Clint wrapped an arm around her and pulled her closer to him so he didn't have to yell. "You raise your voice any more and whatever good you did with those gamblers will be ruined."

When she looked over to the card table she'd left be-hind, Mia didn't so much as wobble. When she looked back, a good amount of the drunkenness seemed to have evaporated. "All right then," she said in a fairly steady voice. "How about we place a wager?"

"Are you pretending to be drunk?" Clint asked.

"Don't change the subject, Mr. Adams."

"All right," Clint said, while looking at her with a new level of respect. "What's the wager?"

"I'll bet you five hundred dollars that I wind up winning more than you do on the *Misty Morning*."

"You want to lose another five hundred on top of everything else? Be my guest."

"Is it a wager or not?"

Clint held a hand out to her. "Let's make it official."

"Sealing it with a handshake?" she asked. "I was thinking more along the lines of this." Leaning in, Mia pressed her lips against Clint's and held them there as she wrapped her arms around him.

Her lips were hot and became even hotter the longer Clint felt them. Just as they were about to sear into him, he opened his mouth to take a breath and immediately felt Mia's mouth open as well. Their tongues met briefly before they eased back to catch their breath for real.

Clint's erection had been growing the moment the kiss had started. Now Mia was shifting her hips back and forth to make it grow even harder.

"Since you feel like upping the ante," Clint said, "why not make it even more interesting?"

NINE

Clint hadn't gotten a very good look at the room he'd rented at the Boathouse. In fact, he'd simply made sure the key fit, dumped his saddlebags on the floor and left to get something to drink. Now that he was coming back to it, he got even less of a look at what kind of room he'd gotten for his money.

He and Mia practically fell through the doorway. They weren't too drunk to walk, but were tangled in each other's arms as they struggled to pull off each other's clothes while moving into the room. Mia was getting the upper hand on that account and had already pulled open Clint's shirt and started to unbuckle his jeans.

Clint, on the other hand, had just managed to loosen the laces holding the front of her dress shut.

"And you said I was the drunk one," Mia chuckled as she squirmed to make herself more readily available to Clint's eager fingers. "You're about to ruin a brand-new dress."

After saying that, Mia took a slow step back and ran her hand down the laces along the front of the top of her dress. Her free hand snapped forward and might have knocked Clint across the room if he hadn't fallen onto the bed. Her

31

strength was a surprise, but not an unwelcome one. As
much as he liked the show of force, Clint didn't like the
fact that he could no longer see her too well in the dark
room.

As if reading his mind, Mia reached out to the closest
lamp and twisted the knob. The flame grew just bright
enough to fill the room with a dull glow. There were pic-
tures on the walls of various riverboats, and the furniture
was actually pretty nice. None of that held Clint's interest,
however. The only reason he looked at all was to see what
kind of space he had to work with.

Mia leaned against the wall and arched her back as she
slowly pulled open the laces of her bodice. The velvet
came open, but clung to her skin as if it didn't want to let
her go. Running her hands up over her breasts, Mia slid
them down so her fingernails caught on the top edge of the
material. She closed her eyes and smiled, and she eased
the velvet down to reveal her pert breasts and dark little
nipples.

Clint was enjoying the show, but he was unable to keep
himself in his spot much longer. He worked his way to the
edge of the bed and sat so he could reach for her with both
hands. The moment he got close enough to feel the velvet
against his fingertips, he was smacked away by Mia's
quick hand.

"Not so fast, cowboy," she said.

He'd barely felt the slap on his wrist, but Clint could
feel the ache of not being able to touch her through his entire body. As Mia eased the velvet down even farther to
show him the tight contour of her stomach, Clint reached
for her again.

Mia let him slide his hand along her side and even allowed him to move that hand up toward her breast. The
moment he reached out to cup her with both hands, Mia
grabbed his wrists and pushed him away again. That

brought Clint to his feet, and she immediately moved to the other side of the room.

"You're testing me," Clint said as he pulled off his shirt.

She grinned back at him and nodded. "You think so?" As soon as Clint moved toward her, Mia's eyes flared with the challenge of trying to elude him in the small room. She wound up in front of a high-backed chair and yelped a bit when she felt her legs bump against it.

Now Clint was smiling as he stood in front of her and reached out to take her in his arms. "You've got nowhere else to go now," he whispered.

Mia tried to wriggle away, but didn't try nearly hard enough to actually shake free. She moved her mouth up to his and waited until Clint kissed her to make her next move. Grabbing hold of his belt, she used it to spin him around so he now had his back to the chair.

Their eyes met and locked onto one another. Clint pulled her close, but didn't kiss her. Instead, he savored the heat of her body so close to him. Her dress was so loose on her now that all he had to do was move an arm to get the material to slide down farther along her body.

Mia writhed in Clint's grasp as if she was trying to deny him another kiss. What she actually did was shed her dress like a snake crawling out of its own skin. When the velvet was collected around her waist, Mia took Clint's wrists again and guided them the rest of the way down.

Her dress fell to the floor, leaving her naked except for the black boots that were laced almost up to her knee. Keeping hold of Clint's wrists, she pushed him back against the chair. Clint dropped onto the chair and kicked off his jeans so Mia could settle on top of him.

"Now," Mia purred as she reached down to guide Clint's penis between her legs, "I've got you right where I want you."

Clint kept his hands on her hips and held his breath as

the tip of his cock found its way inside of her. He let his breath out slowly as she lowered herself onto him. As he slipped all the way inside, he could feel his erection growing until he was hard as a rock.

Mia let out a slow breath as well. When she was all the way down on him, she moved her hands over Clint's bare chest. She got her feet settled on the floor and started pumping her hips back and forth. The moment Clint thrust up into her, Mia let out a loud moan. She leaned forward and ground her hips against his as Clint grabbed onto her tightly with both hands. From there, he gave into the passion that had been building up and pumped into her again and again.

They both caught their breath and stayed still for a few seconds. At that moment, it seemed as if Mia was only just realizing what she was doing. She brushed her hair from her face and looked around. When she looked back down at Clint, she was smiling brightly.

"I wish I could find those men who tried to rob me," she said.

"Why?"

"Because I owe them my thanks." Rocking slowly back and forth, she added, "Without them, I might not have crossed your path."

"I'd rather think about you right now."

Smiling even wider, Mia leaned back and supported her weight with both hands braced on Clint's knees. "That's one hell of a good answer."

"Thank you."

"Don't thank me yet," Mia said as she leaned back and rolled her hips forward and back. She glided up and down along Clint's erection with a rhythm that slowly built in speed and intensity. Soon, she had her eyes closed, her head turned to one side and her hips moving like a piston.

Clint rubbed her breasts with both hands, cupping them as she continued to wriggle on his lap. She leaned forward again to grab the back of the chair on either side of Clint's head. Now that she had a firmer grip, she rode him hard enough to knock the chair against the wall.

Clint wasn't about to let her do all the work. As soon as he felt her slow down, he wrapped his arms around her sweating body and pumped into her again and again.

Mia buried her face against Clint's neck and let out a throaty moan as her entire body was wracked by a powerful orgasm.

Clint could feel her tightening around him. Even her arms clamped around him as if she was clinging at the edge of a cliff. When she was able to catch her breath, Mia started riding him again. This time, she looked down at him so she could watch every second of the pleasure she was giving to him.

Moving his hands from her breasts around to her tight backside, Clint let her keep riding him until his pleasure reached its peak. They moved to the bed and made it a whole half an hour before starting again.

TEN

Clint and Mia both woke up early the next day. It didn't have anything to do with them wanting to get out of bed, since both of them would have been more than happy to stay naked under the sheets for a while longer. Their eyes were opened by the loud knocking on their door.

Sitting bolt upright after the second knock, Clint's first impulse was to look for his gun. The modified Colt was still in reach, exactly where he'd left it. He didn't take the pistol in hand just yet, however, since Mia was slowly sitting up as well.

"Who is that?" she asked.

Apparently, she'd been loud enough to be heard through the door. The knocking stopped and a woman's voice could be heard from the hall.

"Mr. Adams?" the woman outside the room asked.

"Yes," Clint replied.

"Were you waiting for the *Misty Morning*?"

"Yes."

"It's just arriving now."

"All right. Thanks."

There was a quick "You're welcome," followed by shuffling steps away from the door.

Clint kicked off the covers and pulled on his jeans as he made his way to the window. As promised, there was a riverboat approaching the dock.

"Is that the one?" Mia asked excitedly as she stepped up behind Clint.

With the touch of her naked body against his back, it was difficult for Clint to concentrate on the view outside his window. Eventually, he replied, "Probably. I can't see the name on the side, but I think the innkeeper would know better than to wake folks up for a false alarm."

Mia leaned forward a bit more and then quickly pulled back. "It is the *Misty Morning*. I can see the name on the bow."

Clint watched the boat move toward the dock. Standing in the window, he could feel the rays of the early morning sun warming him through the glass. As the boat got closer, men swarmed toward the dock to greet her. In a matter of seconds, the dock appeared to be almost as busy as the saloon had been the night before.

"How long do you think they'll wait?" Mia asked.

"It'll be awhile before they're ready to take anyone on board. You don't have to rush." As he was saying that, Clint turned around to discover Mia was already straightening her dress and cinching up the laces.

The dress didn't look half as good as it had the previous night, but that was mostly because Mia wasn't doing anything more than pulling it over her head and making sure she was fit to walk outside the room. "I need to get my things," she said.

"You didn't bring them in here?"

"When was I going to do that, Clint? We were pretty busy."

"Please don't tell me you left your bags somewhere."

Patting his cheek, she hurried over to the door. "I got my own room, but you're very sweet for worrying about me."

"Not so much worried as sorry that you paid for a room you never used."

"First of all, you're not sorry. Second, I'll be winning plenty of your money to make up for the fee." With that, Mia winked at Clint and rushed through the door.

Clint stayed by the window to watch the men at the dock tend to the riverboat and guide her into position. Ropes were thrown, knots were tied and commands were shouted back and forth. All of it may as well have been in a foreign language as far as Clint was concerned, but it was still interesting to watch.

What was even more interesting was the sight of the people gathered across from the dock. There were several men and women standing next to their bags, chatting among themselves or simply observing one another. Clint had no trouble recalling every face he could spot as someone from the saloon the night before. The ones who caught his attention the most were the gamblers who took the time to turn and look toward the Boathouse.

One of those men spotted Clint immediately and tipped his hat.

Clint gave the man an offhanded wave and stepped away from the window.

"I guess it's time to meet the competition," Clint said to himself.

ELEVEN

In the space of a few minutes, the entire street had changed. When Clint had first walked over to his window, the approaching riverboat was one of the only things in sight that was moving. In the short amount of time it had taken for Clint to get dressed and walk downstairs, the whole place was alive and kicking.

The Boathouse was filled with smells of breakfast being cooked and workers preparing for business to pick up. Outside, shop owners opened their doors and put on a friendly smile for the new faces who gathered along the boardwalk. Clint watched all of these things happen as he made his way to the street to get a closer look at the newest arrival for himself.

The *Misty Morning* arrived as if it had been named for this very moment. The water was coated with a fine layer of fog as the warm rays of the sun met up with a river that had been chilled by the night. The paddle wheel wasn't moving, so it took plenty of strong arms to pull the boat the few extra inches it needed to bump against the dock. Once there, a plank was lowered and more ropes were tied off.

From the window in his room, Clint thought that several of the people watching the boat were chatting to one another. Now that he was on street level, he could feel the air for himself and could smell the tension crackling between the gamblers as if a storm was about to set in.

The gamblers tended to stick to the groups they'd formed the night before. Clint noticed right away that the people who'd played at the same tables stayed together now. Their laughter wasn't exactly friendly, however, since most of them were still sizing one another up. When they weren't talking to one another, the groups were staring down other groups and exchanging a few guarded nods or tips of the hat.

The door to the Boathouse swung open and Mia stepped outside. She was wearing a pale yellow dress with a white ribbon tied around her waist. "Did I miss anything?"

"No," Clint replied, "but it seems like you weren't the only one starting your game early."

"What's that mean?"

"I'd think twice about whatever you thought you learned from these people during last night's game. They're all circling each other so much right now, I'd be surprised if every last one of them isn't dizzy."

Mia swatted Clint's arm and said, "Oh, last night was just a friendly game."

Clint looked over to her and grinned.

"What's got you so happy?" she asked as some of his grin found its way to her face.

"I'm just thinking about how I'm going to spend all that money I'll win from our bet."

"Keep dreaming." With that, Mia brushed her hair back behind both ears and strutted past Clint to make her way to the nearest group of gamblers. Like most of the others, she started off with the men she'd played against the night before. Unlike the others, she quickly moved along to introduce herself to the other groups.

Clint had no problem staying where he was and watching Mia work. Her yellow dress wasn't as expensive as the one she'd been in before, but it hugged her cute little body nicely. Knowing exactly what was under that dress made it even easier to watch her bounce from one group to the next.

It wasn't long before Clint was aware that he was being watched.

That wasn't much of a surprise, considering the company he was in, but Clint knew it was potentially dangerous to give folks the wrong impression at this early stage of the game. Thinking back to what Mia had tried to do in last night's game, Clint kept his eyes on her and didn't acknowledge the eyes that were on him until the last possible second.

Twitching a bit in surprise as the man approached him, Clint thought he put on just enough of a show to make himself look distracted and possibly even a little nervous.

"Good morning, there," the man said as he approached Clint. He looked to be in his early thirties, but could have been a bit younger. A youthful face combined with an expensive, tailored suit made it tough to judge his age any better than that.

Clint shook the man's hand and said, "Hello. I didn't see you coming."

"Late night?"

"I think all of us at that saloon had a late night."

The man chuckled and took a cigarette case from his jacket pocket. He opened it and held it out to Clint. After he was refused, he took a cigarette for himself and struck a match to light it. "I've seen better places for cards, but you couldn't beat the company."

"I hear that."

"Really? Then why didn't you play?"

Clint looked over to him and studied the man for a few seconds. There was an edge in the man's steely eyes that said he knew he was being watched and didn't give a damn.

"I'm saving my money for the real games," Clint said while nodding toward the riverboat.

"Every game could possibly be the biggest game of your life. If anyone would know that, I would think Clint Adams would."

Nodding to confirm the name the other man had thrown out, Clint said, "Then maybe I just didn't want to go broke before stepping onto such a fine new boat."

The man looked toward the dock and pulled in a deep breath. The cigarette in his mouth flared, and soon smoke was drifting from his nostrils. "She does look like a new boat, doesn't she?" Suddenly shifting around, the man said, "By the way, my name is—"

"Jean Claude Vessele," Clint said.

This time, it was the other man's turn to look surprised. In his case, he seemed to be genuinely caught off his guard. Either that, or he was just a much better actor than Clint. "I wouldn't have thought I would be known to a man such as you," he said.

"Anyone who wins a hundred thousand dollars and a hundred acres of California property from the same man in the same game is going to be well known," Clint pointed out.

Jean Claude shrugged, grinned and puffed on his cigarette. "That was a hell of a game. I should say a hell of a lucky game."

"Sure it was," Clint replied. "Luck could account for one win like that, but not as many as you've had. I heard there was a game in Alaska that left you owning half of a mountain."

Jean Claude kept a straight face, but not for very long. He shook his head and gripped his cigarette in the corner of his mouth so he could once again shake Clint's hand. "Mr. Adams, you have the ears of a hawk and the memory of an elephant. Remind me to give you a wide berth. I believe you're the first I've met in over a year who knows about that game."

"Hopefully, that wide berth doesn't apply to the card table," Clint said.

"Did you bring money with you?"

"Of course."

"Then it doesn't apply," Jean Claude said with a wink. "Now, if you'll excuse me, it looks as if the *Misty Morning* is accepting passengers."

Clint looked over to the dock. From what he saw, it looked less like a boat taking on passengers and more like a pile of fresh beef being revealed to a pack of hungry wolves. Rather than wade into the flood of gamblers making their way to the single plank, Clint hung back and counted the number of faces he recognized.

TWELVE

The *Misty Morning* was a new boat. Clint didn't have to be an experienced sailor to know that much. All he needed was a pair of eyes and a nose to see that the boards in the floor barely even had a scuff on them and still smelled as if they'd just been cut off the tree. There were plenty of riverboats that were bigger. Even the one that had been docked there the night before was plenty bigger. The *Misty Morning* was made for gamblers, however. Anyone else needed to step off the deck before all their money disappeared.

The *Misty Morning* was also a very crowded boat. As soon as Clint walked onboard, he was around so many people that he couldn't stretch his arms out in any direction. Men in expensive suits were constantly bumping into him. Women in fancy dresses were stepping around him. Needless to say, Clint spent a lot of time guarding his pockets.

"Have you been greeted, sir?"

Clint turned to face the source of the smooth, deep voice that he'd just heard. Considering how many people were around, he figured the odds were pretty bad that the voice had been speaking to him. When he spotted the well-dressed man with the salt-and-pepper hair, Clint was surprised to find that the man was waiting for an answer.

44

"Oh," Clint said. "You're talking to me?"

"Yes, sir."

The man looked to be in his fifties. His black and gray hair was neatly trimmed and stayed perfectly in place. The mustache on his narrow lip was so thin that it seemed to have been drawn there by a swipe of a pencil. He wore a plain black suit, which somehow stood out from all the other plain black suits milling about.

"Have you been greeted?" the man asked.

"I don't believe so."

"Then allow me to welcome you aboard the *Misty Morning.* Your accommodations are provided for you and your room number is at the bottom of your invitation. You do still have your invitation, don't you?"

"Yes, I do."

Hearing that was enough to break the expressionless mask that had been on the older man's face until then. "Excellent. May I see it?"

Clint reached into his pocket and produced the invitation.

Seeing that he hadn't been bluffed after all, the older man smiled and let out the breath that had been forcing him to stand as if there was an iron rod running along the back of his jacket. He tapped a small number written at the bottom of the invitation that Clint hadn't even noticed before. "There it is, sir. You'll find that room toward the rear of the boat."

Clint folded the invitation again and stuffed it into his pocket. "A lot of these people didn't bring their invitations, huh?"

"You would be amazed."

"Well, it'll probably make you feel better to know that plenty of these men will be losing their shirts and most everything they own on this boat."

The man didn't answer, but he wore a real warm smile on his face as he walked away to greet the next gambler.

Clint found himself pushed in the general direction of

the railing, so he stood there and looked over the side at the dock. Even though he was a stone's throw from the Boathouse, he felt as if he was already miles away. The street looked even smaller from this angle and the river looked a whole lot bigger.

A whistle blew from higher up near the smokestacks, and Clint thought he felt something within the riverboat start to shift. It was at that moment he realized how long it had been since he'd seen Mia. For all he knew, she could have been somewhere below the deck or even off the boat entirely.

"Aw dammit," Clint groaned as he recalled Mia saying she still had some things in a room at the Boathouse. If the *Misty Morning* was going to leave soon, Mia could get left behind.

As Clint worked his way toward the gangplank, he saw a younger man working his way up from the dock. There were bags stuffed under each arm and one dangling from his hand. Clint was about to try to get past the heavily burdened fellow, but he felt someone push past him instead.

"Watch yourself," Mia said as she hurried down the plank. She waved for the young man and then pushed Clint back onto the boat. "Where do you think you're going? I think the boat's about to leave."

"I was going to try and find you."

"Aww," she said while patting his cheek. "That's sweet."

"Is that stuff yours?" Clint asked.

"Yes. There's no way I could carry it all, and you disappeared before I could ask you."

"All of it's yours?"

"Yes."

"You barely had enough to fill one saddlebag."

"I told you I went shopping," she said impatiently. "You didn't seem to mind the dress I bought. Why should I even have to explain this to you?"

Clint held up his hands as if to surrender the point,

while also getting out of the younger man's way. "No need to explain anything. I just didn't know you bought out half the store."

"Are you worried about my money?"

"Now that I know you're on board, I'm not worried about a thing."

"That's more like it," she said.

Although there were still way too many people wandering around the upper deck of the boat, there were no more coming up the gangplank. After the next whistle blew, the *Misty Morning* started to rumble as the paddle wheel began to turn.

Mia had already found her way to the older man in the black suit.

"Hello, ma'am," the man said. "Have you been greeted?"

"No, I haven't," Mia replied cheerily.

"Do you have your invitation?"

"I had it awhile ago, but I think I may have misplaced it."

The older man rolled his eyes and let out a weary sigh.

THIRTEEN

The *Misty Morning* pulled away from the dock and floated down the Red River. Clint stayed on the top deck and watched the dock drift away and the river widen in front of them. From what he'd heard, there were to be a few more stops that day and then they wouldn't be stopping until it was time to let people off.

It did strike Clint as a bit odd that the boat wasn't going to make any stops along the way, but he doubted any of the gamblers would want to get off anyhow. Ever since they'd all swarmed the decks and gotten a look at their competition, nearly all the passengers had disappeared inside the boat. Clint remained where he was, leaned against the rail, and filled his lungs with the fragrant river air.

Behind him, Clint could hear the tapping of light footsteps moving toward the rail.

"It's so quiet out here," a woman said.

Clint turned around to find a tall blonde in a cream-colored dress settling against the rail. Her long hair flowed into wavy curls that reminded Clint of decorative ribbons wrapped around a Christmas present. Her skin was smooth and fair. The lilt in her voice along with the parasol she propped on one shoulder gave her a distinctly Southern flair.

"Aren't you here to play cards?" she asked.

Clint nodded and turned so he was leaning back against the rail. "Sure, but there's plenty of time for that later. Besides, it's kind of nice to breathe in a few times without filling up with smoke."

"It is rather foggy in the main room."

"I take it the games are already starting?" Clint asked.

"Oh, my yes. I doubt they'll be ending anytime soon."

"You must have traveled a bit to get here. Georgia, was it?"

The blonde blinked once and stepped back as if Clint had just read her future. "Why, yes. How did you know?"

"The accent says it all."

She narrowed her eyes, studied him and then tapped her chin with her finger. "You're not from Texas because you don't talk like a cowboy. You're not from Oklahoma. I've heard plenty of accents from around there." After a few seconds, she said, "Actually, I'm bad at this. You could be from anywhere for all I know."

"Anywhere and everywhere. My name's Clint."

Content not to question him any further on the subject, the blonde shook the hand Clint offered and said, "I'm Gretchen Bowes."

"Pleased to meet you, Gretchen."

"Likewise I'm sure," she replied as she added a little curtsy as if it was second nature. "So you are here to gamble?"

"If I was here to steer the boat, I'd sure be standing in the wrong place."

Gretchen's laughter was as pretty as it was promising. "I suppose that was a silly question."

"What about you?" Clint asked. "Are you a gambler?"

"I dabble, but it was my sister who received the invitation."

"Your sister?"

"Yes," Gretchen said with a nod. "She's the wild one of

the family. She used to play cards with our daddy, and
when she walked into a saloon to play for real money, she
never looked back."

"Since she's the wild one," Clint said, "I suppose that
makes you the beautiful one?"

Although a blush didn't actually show on her cheeks,
Gretchen averted her eyes and covered her face with her
hand as if it did. "Stop it," she said as she moved a little
closer. "We've only just met."

"Sorry. All this river air must be getting to me. Perhaps
we should get out of it before something happens."

Gretchen gave a look of genuine surprise as she slowly
lowered her hand from her mouth. Her full, red lips were
parted as if to speak, but she didn't get a chance to say a
word.

"Would you be able to escort me into the main room?"
Clint asked as he held out an arm. "I wouldn't want to get
lost and walk into the furnace by mistake."

Shifting her surprised expression into a smile, Gretchen
nodded and looped her arm around Clint's. "I wouldn't
mind one bit," she said. "I think this river air was getting to
me, too."

With a few practiced moves, Gretchen closed her parasol and swung it down so she could use it like a cane in her
free hand. She fell into step next to Clint and timed her
steps perfectly so her well-rounded hip bumped slightly
against him as they walked.

The closer Clint got to the door leading down into the
boat, the more the quiet, outside world faded away. The
sounds of splashing water and chirping birds was quickly
replaced by dozens of voices, glasses rattling against one
another and a piano playing a steady stream of Chopin.

Clint and Gretchen walked down a single flight of stairs
which led them into a large room filled with card tables
arranged in perfect rows, with chairs set up perfectly
around them. Nearly every one of those chairs was full, but

Clint still felt as if he was missing something as he looked around the room.

"There must be fewer games started than I thought," he said. "This only looks like about half the people that were on the deck before."

"That deck looked positively chaotic." Gretchen sighed. "But there wasn't this much space up top, you know. That made it seem like twice the number of people milling about."

"Yeah, but there's still got to be plenty more people in their rooms."

"Or they could be in one of the other poker rooms," she offered.

"There are more poker rooms?"

She nodded. "Two more. One at the front of the boat and one at the back. They're not as big as this one, though."

Clint had already spotted Mia sitting at one of the tables closest to the bar. She waved and shot him a look that was practically a command for him to approach her. "We might as well start here, I suppose," he said.

"I'm going to find my sister." Gretchen said as she stepped away from him. Brushing her hand along Clint's cheek, she added, "I'll find you later."

"I sure hope so."

Clint watched Gretchen turn around and head for one of the other doors leading out of the room. Even though she wore more than a few layers under her petticoat, the swaying of her hips was still easy to distinguish. When he finally took his eyes off the pleasant sight, Clint found Mia glaring at him with more than a little venom in her eyes.

Smiling and walking over to her, Clint tugged on the collar of his rumpled shirt as if that would make a difference in his appearance. "I feel a little underdressed for this place," he said once he got to where Mia was sitting.

Her table was only half-full. One of the men was in his sixties and had a bushy set of muttonchops running along the sides of his face. The bristly hair barely even moved as he grumbled, "Only a little underdressed?"

Clint wanted to answer back, but the man had room to talk since he was sporting a tailored black suit complete with a gold watch chain crossing his belly.

"Who was that?" Mia asked.

"I don't know," Clint replied. "I didn't catch the gentleman's name."

"Not him. The blonde. Who was she?"

"I'm going to my room. We can discuss this when I get back." Clint put his back to the table, walked away and hoped Mia would have forgotten about her question by the time he returned.

FOURTEEN

"Damn," Clint muttered as he looked at himself in the mirror in his room.

He knew the suit he'd brought wasn't going to surpass anything worn by some of those well-dressed gamblers in the main room. He didn't have much space to pack a wardrobe into his saddlebags and would have been more than satisfied with the clothes he did bring. What he couldn't bear was the thought of walking into that gambling room wearing something that looked as if it had been dragged through the mud.

Clint stood in front of that mirror and took a moment to think if he had dragged that suit through the mud. He then looked down at himself and at the wrinkled mess that was the suit he wore. He couldn't recall what the hell he'd done to it, but that suit wasn't even an improvement over the battered jeans and rumpled shirt he'd had on before.

One quick change later, Clint walked out of his room with a bundle of clothes tucked under his arm. He made his way toward the upper deck, but didn't have to go all the way to the stairs before he spotted the man he'd been looking for.

"Can I help you, sir?" the man with the salt-and-pepper

hair asked as he turned around before Clint had to catch his attention.

"Yes, I was wondering if there's a laundry or anything like that on this boat."

"On the lower deck toward the back, sir. May I accompany you?"

"If you could just point me in the right direction, that should be fine."

The older man held up one gloved hand, extended one long finger and pointed that finger toward the back of the boat. "You'll find the stairs that way, sir."

"Let me guess," Clint said. "I want the ones going down?"

"Precisely."

For some reason, Clint found himself chuckling at the way the older man's expression didn't falter in the slightest. "You should be a card player with that face."

"I'll take it under advisement."

Clint started to walk down the hall, but stopped and asked, "Next time I've got a stupid question, who should I ask for?"

"Does it have to be me?"

"Yep."

"Then you would ask for Arvin."

"I'll keep that in mind."

Clint watched for another roll of the eyes from the older man, but Arvin simply remained in his spot until he knew that Clint was walking in the proper direction. After that, he continued down the hall.

The stairs leading down into the lowest level weren't nearly as nice as the ones that Clint had used so far. In fact, they seemed likely to crack under his feet as he made his way down with nothing more than a rope strung through some brass loops to steady him.

He didn't have to go far before he heard several voices chattering amid the rumble of the paddle wheel and ruckus of the furnace room. All Clint had to do was follow the acrid scent of starch emanating from one of the narrow doors to find the one marked "Laundry." Once there, Clint knocked and waited.

Some of the voices Clint heard stopped the moment his knuckles rapped against the door. Leaning in close to the door, Clint could make out frantic whispering coming from the next room.

"Hello?" Clint said. "I've got some clothes that need some help."

There was no reply.

"I can pay for the services," Clint added. "I just need the job done quickly."

When he heard one faint voice cut short by a gruff obscenity, Clint reached down and tried the handle of the door. The door wasn't locked, but Clint wasn't about to just throw it open and step inside. His hand drifted toward the Colt at his side, but he didn't draw the pistol just yet. Instead, he shifted the clothes to his gun hand so they covered the Colt as well as a good portion of his gun belt. Then, Clint opened the door.

Three women were huddled in a corner of the small room. One of them was Chinese, and she was the only one who wasn't too petrified to move. She stood up and extended an arm to point at Clint while staring at him with wide, terrified eyes.

In the space of a heartbeat, Clint realized two things.

The first thing was that the woman wasn't pointing directly at him but at the doorway.

The second was that there was someone lunging at Clint from where they must have been waiting with their back against the wall in the very spot where the woman was pointing.

FIFTEEN

Clint turned on the balls of his feet and brought up his arm just in time to catch the arm of the man who'd lunged at him from the doorway. At first, Clint thought he'd just deflected a punch, but he quickly saw the glint of the blade gripped in the other man's fist. The only thing that kept the blade from drawing Clint's blood was the fact that his suit was still wrapped around his arm.

Seeing that knife poised an inch or so from his face gave Clint more than enough strength to push the man's arm away.

"Who the hell are you?" the man asked as he backed up a step and crouched with his knife switching from hand to hand.

Clint took a few cautious sidesteps as he put himself between the man and the women cowering against the far wall. "I just needed a suit cleaned. You've got a bit more to explain."

The man with the knife was short and lean. His skin was deathly pale, and he moved as if the knife was an extension of his own arm. "I don't need to explain anything to a dead man!" he said as he swapped the knife into his right hand and made a low stab at Clint.

Clint reflexively sucked in his gut and arched his back so he could avoid as much of the blade as possible without giving the man enough room to make a quick follow-up swipe. As soon as the blade passed by him, Clint swung down the arm wrapped up in his suit and slammed the man's knife hand against the wall.

While trying to get his hand free, the man twisted his body so his other arm could get a solid shot at Clint's ribs. Bony knuckles slammed against Clint's side, snapped back and jabbed in again before Clint had a chance to react.

Every muscle in Clint's torso tensed to absorb the punches. The man's fist didn't do any real damage, but it hurt like hell as it cracked into the exact same spot three times in a row. Not wanting to let the man's knife arm loose, Clint rolled along the trapped arm and drove his elbow into the man's face.

That knocked the man flat against the wall to slam the door shut. What caught Clint's attention the most was the sound of the knife rattling against the floor. Before he could do anything about it, however, Clint lost sight of the other man altogether.

The man got away from Clint like a greased pig and almost got behind him before Clint turned and threw another elbow at the only spot the man could have gone. Sure enough, Clint's elbow hit something solid after traveling only an inch or two. He'd put enough muscle behind it to make a satisfying crunch on impact.

"Look out!" one of the ladies screamed.

Clint wheeled around in the same direction as he'd thrown the last elbow. The smaller man had already moved from that spot and dropped down to sweep the knife up off the floor.

Rather than try to switch the direction his arm was swinging, the other man spun his entire body around. When he'd made a complete, tight circle, he brought his arm around and snapped it out like a whip. This time, Clint knew better than to try and just lean out of the way. He saw that blade coming toward him and jumped back before it cut right through him.

The sharpened steel whistled through the air. Clint could feel a cold breeze as the blade swiped past his neck. For a moment, Clint wasn't even sure if he'd been cut. He reached up to press a hand to his throat and felt his stomach drop when he felt something wet against his fingers.

Pulling his hand down, Clint quickly took a look and saw nothing more than sweat on his hand. When he looked up again, the smaller man already had the door partially open.

"Oh no you don't," Clint grunted as he rushed forward.

The man gritted his teeth and lashed out with the blade once to stop Clint in his tracks. He kept slashing quick patterns through the air to get Clint to keep his distance. Dark, burning eyes fixed upon Clint and watched every little move he made. The instant he saw Clint go for his gun, the man made a forward stab aimed for Clint's wrist.

Clint reflexively jumped back. Even though it was only one step, it was enough to knock his heel against a basket of clothes on the floor. He took half a second to look behind him and regain his balance, which was enough for the other man to slip through the door and out into the hall.

Keeping his hand on the Colt's grip and ready to draw in the blink of an eye, Clint moved to the door and extended an arm to push it open. Just as his fingertips made contact with the wooden surface, he felt a solid thump against the wall. When he tried to open the door, it wouldn't budge.

Clint took half a step back and then slammed his shoulder against the door hard enough to knock it off its hinges. Fortunately, the broom that had been wedged against the door from the outside snapped in two before the hinges gave way. Stumbling into the hall with his gun held at the ready, Clint looked around for a target.

The narrow hall was empty on both sides, but he soon heard commotion coming from the direction of the stairs. Clint rushed that way and found several doors open and several heads poking out.

"Did you see anyone rush past here?" Clint asked.

The heads eventually all shook and the faces looked at Clint with growing nervousness.

Clint stood in the hall and listened for a sign of where he should go next. He heard nothing, so he holstered the Colt and walked up and down the hall. The few doors there were already open, and the rooms were wide-open storage areas or places where people were doing their work. Those people were all either hiding the man or didn't have the first clue where he went. Either way, Clint knew he'd hit a dead end.

After making his way back to the laundry, Clint checked on the three women. "Are you ladies all right?" he asked.

They nodded.

"Do you know who that was?"

"No," the Chinese woman replied. "He was in here poking around and threatened to kill us. That's when you came here. You saved our lives," she added while hugging Clint around the waist. "How can I thank you?"

"Well," he said, while looking down at the rumpled pile of clothes on the floor, "it looks like I could use a new suit."

SIXTEEN

When Clint returned to the main card room, Mia didn't even recognize him. She did turn to watch him enter, but her eyes lingered on his as if she couldn't quite place where she'd seen him before. Once she got a better look at his face, she got up and rushed over to him.

"Clint? I barely recognized you!" she said.

He wore a black suit complete with tailored cuffs and a jacket with tails that nearly reached down to his heels. Still straightening the collar, he replied, "I barely recognized myself when I got a look at this thing."

"I didn't think you'd be the sort to have a suit like that."

"I'm not. I'm only wearing this until my own suit is stitched up."

"What happened to it?" she asked.

"It's a long story. This place looks a lot busier than when I was last here."

Mia's hand lingered on Clint's arm as if she didn't even realize it was there, but a part of her didn't want to let him go. "You should see the other rooms," she said while taking a look around. "They're so full, it's a wonder this thing stays afloat. All the big games are in here for now, though."

"That'll change later tonight. The big money has a way of seeking out the smaller rooms."

"Sounds like a man with plenty of experience."

Clint shrugged and gave up on trying to feel comfortable inside the expensive suit. Even though the clothes had been freshly cleaned and were waiting to be picked up by their owner, Clint couldn't help but feel like he wanted to crawl out of them and get back into his old jeans. "You didn't happen to hear about some little fellow running around with a knife, did you?"

Mia furrowed her brow and replied, "No. Why do you ask?"

"Another long story. Since I didn't come here to tell stories," Clint said as he rubbed his hands together anxiously, "I might as well get down to business."

Before Clint could take two steps, he was stopped by a large man who stepped in front of him like a massive door being swung shut in Clint's face. The big man was built like a fort, but dressed better than most everyone else in the room. In fact, his suit looked suspiciously similar to the one Clint was wearing.

"You can't go in there like that," the big man snarled.

"It's all right," Clint said. "I have an invitation."

But the big man didn't move. "No guns allowed."

"There wasn't a problem before."

"That was before. This is now."

Mia shrugged and said, "They came through while you were away and took everyone's guns. With this many card games going on, it only makes sense."

Normally, Clint wouldn't have a problem leaving his gun behind. In fact, he could see the logic behind the request very easily. Considering he'd just been attacked not too long ago on this very boat, handing over his weapon wasn't such an easy thing for Clint to do. But the big man obviously wasn't going to make an exception for him, so Clint unbuckled his gun belt and handed it over.

The big man took the weapon, draped the belt over his arm and handed Clint a slip of paper with a number on it. "You can claim it whenever you leave, but there won't be any more guns allowed in any card room."

"What about knives?" Clint asked. "Have you had any problems with knives being swung around here?"

The man didn't even flinch when he heard the question. He simply replied, "No knives allowed, either. If you have one, you should hand it over."

"What if things get out of line?" Clint asked. "Some gamblers do tend to cheat, you know."

The big man smirked and moved an arm to reveal the double-rig shoulder holster strapped beneath his jacket. "Anyone that steps out of line will be real sorry."

"I guess that'll have to do," Clint said.

Once he had what he was after, the big man stepped aside and let Clint pass. Mia fell into step beside Clint and took his arm.

"What's wrong with you?" she whispered. "Did something happen that I should know about?"

But Clint's eyes were already roaming over the room full of poker tables. As he looked for any trace of the man who'd had the knife, he found himself also studying the gamblers. With so many people there and so many more on the boat, Clint knew that looking for the man with the knife was like searching for a needle in a very big haystack.

"I'm just anxious to get into a game," he said to Mia. "Do you have any suggestions on where I should start?"

She smiled and nodded toward her own table. "I've been saving you a seat."

"Great. Why don't you let everyone know I'm coming and I'll get something to drink."

"All right."

When Mia left, Clint walked over to the big fellow who'd taken his guns. The man was taking Clint's gun belt to a narrow room guarded by more gunmen, who saw Clint coming right away. Clint held up his hands and approached the man he'd spoken to already.

"Is anyone expecting trouble on this boat?" Clint asked.

The big man shook his head and crossed his arms now that he'd passed off Clint's gun belt. "It's just like you said before. Gamblers tend to get cross when they play too long together. This is all just a precaution."

"Whose precaution?"

"Pardon me?"

"Who's running this tournament?"

"Just have a seat and play some cards," the big man said. "Leave the rest to us."

"Someone may have stowed away," Clint said. "And I don't think it was just so he could sit in on a game."

That caused all the gunmen to straighten up and take notice. Their hands drifted toward their pistols, making Clint feel practically naked since his gun wasn't even in his possession. There were alternatives to having a gun at his side, however. Otherwise, he never would have let the modified Colt out of his hands.

"Where's the stowaway?" the big man asked.

"I ran into someone down in the laundry," Clint explained. "Ask the women down there and they'll tell you all about it."

The big man who'd taken Clint's gun glanced to one of the others nearby. That and a nod was all that was needed to get one of those men heading for the door. Turning back to Clint, the bigman said, "We'll look into it. Anything else you want to tell us?"

"Just that he's dangerous and good with a knife."

"Thank you. Good luck with your game."

Clint walked toward Mia's table. Around so many strangers, he didn't want to bring up what had happened, since the guards seemed to have things well in hand. Now Clint just needed to figure out why nobody had asked what the stowaway looked like or where he was headed.

One possibility was that the guards were overly confident that they could find anyone who didn't belong on the riverboat.

Another possibility was that they already knew about the man with the knife. Either way, Clint decided to keep what he'd seen under his hat until he was talking to someone he knew he could trust. On a riverboat full of poker players, something like that might be a little hard to come by.

SEVENTEEN

The ace of spades flipped around the man's perfectly manicured fingers like a leaf that had caught a subtle breeze. It drifted in his grasp for a few seconds, landed in his palm and then was effortlessly tossed onto the table in front of him.

A knock came from his door, rattling through the small cabin like a clap of thunder.

"Come on in," he said casually as his left hand drifted toward the gun secreted in his pocket.

The door opened, and the skinny knife fighter hurried inside. His stringy hair clung to his face, and a grin was plastered upon his mouth. As soon as he was inside, he closed the door to a narrow crack and positioned himself so he could stare through the crack at the narrow hallway outside.

"You smell terrible, Dench," the well-dressed man sitting at the table said. "Even worse than usual, and that's saying a lot."

Without moving from his spot, Dench shook his head and spoke in a rasping whisper. "I had to spend some time in the laundry."

"That explains the smell. It doesn't explain why you're so late."

"Not all of us got to walk on board like everyone else. You set up this fucking boat ride, Jack. How come I couldn't just walk onto the damn boat like a human being?"

The man sitting at the table froze in his spot. His hand had moved away from his gun and was now occupied with the game of solitaire he'd been playing before Dench's arrival. He had a full head of thick, black hair which hung around his face as if every strand was arranged as intricately as the clothes he wore.

An expensive silk suit was draped perfectly over broad shoulders and came complete with every accessory money could buy. Gold cuff links, a gold watch and a gold tie tack all matched one another perfectly. There were a few scars on his face, but even those seemed to be there to make him look a bit more dashing.

"I didn't set up this trip," the handsome man said. "And I don't appreciate my employees calling me by my common name."

Dench's first impulse was to turn away from the door with a disgusted sneer etched onto his face. His hand even started to move toward the knife tucked under his belt, but he stopped once he got a better look at the man seated in front of him.

Even though he hadn't moved more than a few muscles, the well-dressed man had made a slight shift in his manner that made him look less like a gentleman and more like a killer.

After a few seconds of staring death in the face, Dench said, "I just don't see why I had to stow away, Mr. Solomon."

Solomon nodded slowly and looked back down at his cards. "You're a wanted man."

"So are you."

"Yes, but I conduct my business discreetly, whereas you tend to cause a commotion. Case in point, your entrance onto this boat, which was supposed to be nice and quiet."

"It woulda been plenty quiet if I could've just kept my head down and walked on."

Letting out a heavy sigh, Solomon started to set down the remainder of the deck of cards in his hand. Halfway through the motion, he wound up slamming down the cards with enough force to shake up the ones that had already been laid down. "I told you before, I didn't set this whole thing up. I steered a few choice people here and arranged for this to be an accommodating place for us to do our business."

"Anyone that matters knows you're here. All you gotta do is snap yer fingers and I coulda—"

"I swear to Christ if you mention having to stow away one more time, I'll kill you where you stand. There's enough noise on this tub without you yelling about this stupid shit."

Solomon kept his eye on Dench for a few more seconds, until it became clear that Dench wasn't going to push it any further.

"Didn't I tell you there might be some undesirables on board?" Solomon asked in a somewhat soothing tone.

"You mean the law?"

"That's precisely what I mean."

"I thought you were gonna find out about that before this boat even got moving."

Solomon looked down at the table in front of him and began meticulously putting every card exactly where it was supposed to be. "There were some men on the job, but they haven't reported back. We couldn't wait too long for them, so we had to cast off, set sail or whatever the hell else you call it once those damnable paddles start slapping against the water."

Now, Dench took another look out the door. When he closed it this time, he did so very carefully. "How'd the law hear about this?"

"The men we're after aren't exactly unknown to the authorities. They could have been followed or they could have alerted them themselves if they caught wind that I might be here. That's why I couldn't risk you being seen in those few moments when it would have been easiest for someone to turn around and walk straight off this boat."

Reluctantly, Dench said, "I guess that makes sense."

"Now what happened to you? It looks as if you ran into some trouble."

"Someone caught sight of me when I was trying to get out of the goddamn laundry room. I thought I was alone, but some damn Chinese bitch was in there quiet as a church mouse. I meant to shut her up and some asshole walked in on me."

"Is this asshole dead?"

"No."

Solomon nodded and gathered up the cards so they could be shuffled. "Good."

"What the hell do you mean? He could be spreading the word right now, for all we know. He might just flap his lips in front of someone who knows me and then it'll be twice as hard to get done what we came to do."

"Do you know who this person was?" Solomon asked.

"No."

"And does he know who you are?"

Dench thought that over for a second before saying, "I don't think so."

"Then there's no problem. Even if word of your little scuffle gets back to the captain of this boat, all he'll do is send some of the men that were hired to provide security for the gamblers to take a look in the laundry room. I've paid those men enough that they should overlook anything short of a bloodbath under the decks." Fixing his eyes upon Dench, Solomon asked, "They won't find a bloodbath, will they?"

"Not yet."

"Fine. There's no problem, then. We've got one more quick stop to make and then you can spill all the blood you want. Just try to stay out of sight until tomorrow."

"What if that asshole finds me?"

"Then you're not half as good as I think you are, and I'll be better off without you."

Dench watched to see if Solomon was kidding. It was as useless as waiting for a corpse to sneeze.

EIGHTEEN

Clint was sitting at a table with Mia to his left and a portly fellow with a thick red beard to his right. The man with the red beard was named Barry, and he sat with an empty chair on his other side. On the other side of that empty chair was a man in a white suit named Jones.

Since the liquor had started flowing almost as soon as the boat had gotten moving, spirits were high in the large poker room. Women wearing long skirts and low-cut blouses strolled by every few minutes to refill drinks and give the gamblers something to look at when they were sitting out for a hand.

Although Clint knew better than to indulge in too much beer so early in a game, he was enjoying himself even more than he'd anticipated. It seemed all the gamblers were pacing themselves, so the stakes were remaining fairly low and the games were all mostly friendly. He knew that would change once everyone had felt one another out, so Clint enjoyed the calm before the inevitable storm.

"Where's the captain of this ship?" Barry asked.

Being the most straight-faced one at the table, Jones was

quick to reply, "Probably steering or making sure things are running smoothly."

"I just hope he's not drinking along with the rest of these card cheats," Clint added, keeping his tone more in line with Barry's joking nature. "Otherwise it's just a matter of time before we run aground."

Barry lifted his glass as well as his voice. "Here's to the captain!"

Surprisingly enough, those words were met with a round of applause as well as several other glasses raised at several other tables.

Tipping back the large stein, Barry drained some of the beer inside as some more dribbled down his chin to be soaked up by his red beard. "He sure knows how to throw a party!"

"It's your deal," Jones said.

Barry slammed his mug down and wiped his chin like a Viking after pillaging a small village. "Hand over them cards and let me show you how it's done."

Jones slid the deck toward Barry and counted his chips for the tenth time in the last hour. He nodded and then looked around before letting his eyes settle back upon Mia.

Since he'd already seen Jones go through his nervous rituals several times, Clint took a quick look toward the spot where the guards held onto the gamblers' coats and guns. Unlike the previous times he'd looked, Clint now saw the man who'd been sent to check on the situation in the laundry room. He was just finishing speaking with the head guard, who then looked over to Clint as if he knew he was being watched.

The big man met Clint's questioning stare, shook his head and then went about his other business.

"Are you looking for someone?" Mia asked.

Just then, two women entered the room and immediately drew the eyes of everyone else in the place. It would have been impossible to miss them. The blondes walked arm in arm and smiled as if they were greeting every last person, one by one.

The men returned the blondes' smiles with a nod, wave or grin of their own.

The other women in the room weren't quite so glad to see the new arrivals. Mia was no exception.

"Oh," she said dryly. "That's what you were looking at."

Clint meant to deny the accusing tone in her voice at first, but it was difficult to make that seem credible since he was having a hard time taking his eyes off the two blondes. "Actually, I know them," he said.

"You do?" Barry asked. Judging by the excitement in his voice, one might have thought Clint had just claimed to be on speaking terms with the President.

"Well, I know one of them," Clint clarified. "I spoke to her a little while ago. I believe that other one is her sister."

"Sisters, huh?" Barry grunted as he took a moment to let some things drift through his head. "That's even better."

Jones let out a sigh and cleared his throat. "You make me sick. Are you going to deal or not?"

"Aw, you were lookin' too, Jones," Barry said as he began flipping cards to each player.

The woman accompanying Gretchen was close to her height and a bit thinner. Clint guessed the other woman was Gretchen's sister mainly because both women's faces had the same angles and they even walked with a similar confident spring in their step.

The other woman also had blond hair, but with a few hints of red through it. She locked her eyes on Clint almost immediately and leaned over to say something to Gretchen. Although he couldn't hear what the women were saying, Clint knew it was pretty good considering the smiles on both of their faces.

As if that sight wasn't good enough for him, Clint picked up his cards and found that three threes had been dealt to him. "I'm feeling lucky," he said. Ignoring the glare from Mia, he opened the betting by tossing five dollars into the middle of the table.

Mia called the bet and muttered, "It seems like the captain of this boat provided some company for his guests along with the liquor."

Having allowed himself to look back toward the two blondes, Jones realized Mia was staring at him, and he quickly tossed in some money. After looking down at his cards, he even threw in a raise. "Sorry. I was distracted."

"My guess is that's what they're there for, Jones." Barry chuckled. He took a moment to fan his cards and then called the raised bet. "I'm enjoying the show myself."

Clint sat in his chair and focused on the game long enough to appear as if he needed to think about calling, and then tossed in the extra money.

"Go ahead and look, Clint," Mia said. "I'd prefer to have you as distracted as possible. In fact," she added while covering the bet, "you might want to pay for their company. Nobody would blame you."

Discards were tossed toward Barry, and he dealt out the replacements. As those cards were being sent around the table, Clint said, "I didn't come here to buy anyone's company. My guess is that women like that will have more offers than they'd know what to do with."

"Women like what?" a rough yet feminine voice asked from over Clint's shoulder.

Mia smirked and looked at her cards.

Seeing the smug grin on Mia's face, Clint didn't even bother looking over his shoulder to see who'd just spoken. Without looking at his cards, he tossed ten dollars into the pot and said, "We were just discussing the woman's perspective on poker. Some think they're distracting."

"And some of us," Barry said, "just like to be distracted."

Mia rolled her eyes and tossed her cards onto the table. "I'm out."

Jones glanced up and down between his own cards and Clint so many times that he nearly strained something. Before Clint could look at his cards, Jones raised the bet another ten dollars.

"Care to have a seat, ma'am?" Barry asked. "I've got one right next to me with your name on it."

"Call or fold," Jones said impatiently.

After glancing at the one new card he'd gotten, Barry chose the latter and tossed his cards onto Mia's.

Clint still didn't look at his cards before calling the bet. He flipped over the two replacements, found nothing of interest and then showed the three threes. "Medium pair," Clint said as he pointed at Jones. "More than sevens, but no paint. Am I right?"

Jones threw his cards away without showing.

"I think I'll be staying," Gretchen's sister said as she settled into the seat between Jones and Barry.

NINETEEN

Her name was Elsa. When she'd introduced herself, she spoke the name in her deep, sultry voice as though it was a promise for later. She shook each man's hand, saving Mia for last. Even though Mia gave her a bit of a hard stare, Elsa got her to smile with some quick joke that Clint wasn't able to hear.

Mia laughed despite herself and lost the coldness that had been in her eyes when Elsa and Gretchen had first made their entrance. After that, it was all about the cards.

As if to keep the stakes low for a while, no chips were offered at any of the tables. That didn't prevent any of the gamblers from piling stacks of cash in a few pots, but it did keep things in line for the first few hours. The only reason Clint noticed that it had any effect at all was because Jones kept nervously patting his pocket every time he needed to dive in there to pull out some additional funds.

As people started lighting the room with lanterns since there was no longer as much sunlight, Clint found himself sitting behind a fairly good-sized stack of money. Most of it was his own that had been broken down, circulated among the other players and won back again, but some was

75

straight profit. Considering how much fun he'd had, that was a good deal in his eyes.

Gretchen spent a lot of time behind Clint, rubbing his shoulder and whispering into his ear. Most of that was simple conversation, but Clint found he could get under Barry's skin if he acted like Gretchen was saying something a little more interesting.

Elsa and Mia were finding out a lot about their competition as well. Although they'd started off by passing some barbed glances back and forth, they soon were able to lead Barry around by the nose and get him to fold or raise at will. Jones wasn't so easy to sway, which came as a surprise to practically everyone at the table.

For his part, Jones seemed only to be interested in playing his cards. He kept his nose down and stayed out of most of the friendly banter. Although the ladies at the table got a little frustrated with him, Jones provided Clint with plenty of insight that could be put to use later.

Looking down at a busted flush, Clint folded his cards just in time to feel the room move differently around him. "Feels like we're slowing down," he said.

"Stopping is more like it," Barry grunted. "Good time for it, too. I'm about ready to get the hell out of here."

"Oh, don't say that," Elsa purred as she stroked the top of Barry's hand. "I was just getting used to your face."

Barry tried to keep his tough expression intact, but only managed to hold out for a few seconds before grinning. "I was just fooling," he said. "Why the hell would I want to leave a fine table like this? Any chance your sister might come pay me a visit?"

"You just never know," she said with a wink.

Clint could feel the rumble of the water bumping against the side of the boat as the paddle wheel slowed to a halt. The shift in motion wasn't much, but it was noticeable to anyone who was paying the slightest bit of attention.

"Does anyone know how many more stops we're going to be making?" Clint asked.

"Not many," Mia replied. "I think this is the last one."

"Probably to pick up supplies," Jones said. "They were running low on food and such before they made the last stop, but there're only a few more passengers set to board."

Barry stared at Jones with the same mix of surprise and amusement that had been on his face all night when looking at the smaller man. "And just how the hell would you know all that?"

Jones looked around at the others sitting at the table as if he was surprised everyone didn't know that information. Finally, he said, "I asked."

"Well, that explains everything."

Folding his cards and gathering up his money, Clint stood up from the table. By the time his legs were fully straightened, he had the attention of everyone else sitting there.

Although she looked at him with some disappointment, Elsa wasn't laying it on so thick as she had been for Barry when she asked, "Now *you* want to leave?"

"I'm done for this game, but that's only so I can save some money for later," Clint said. "There's still plenty of river ahead of us."

"Good point," Barry said. He then looped an arm around Elsa and added, "Why don't you and me get better acquainted before the big money starts to flow?"

Elsa shrugged off Barry's arm before it even had a chance to settle fully around her. "I'm not going anywhere. In fact, I'm just getting started."

TWENTY

Clint had his money counted by the time he made it to the main door. He considered leaving his gun with the guards, but then remembered what happened the last time he'd wandered the ship on his own. After collecting his Colt, he walked up the stairs and stepped once again into the fresh river air.

"Jesus," he said as he saw the starry sky overhead. He checked his pocket watch, as if the sun was somehow in error rather than his own sense of how much time had passed. Sure enough, it was nearly eight o'clock at night.

The banks of the Red River drifted slowly by as the *Misty Morning* eased forward thanks to the current and its own momentum. They were approaching a small dock that didn't have much of anything connected to it. A few small shacks were scattered along the shore. A pair of wagons also waited there. The passengers of those wagons stepped down and calmly waited for the riverboat to stop.

Clint let his eyes wander as the same set of ropes were cast to allow the passengers to board. When he glanced toward the opposite end of the deck, he saw a slender figure leaning against the rail. The figure was covered in shadow, but slunk away before Clint could get a look at his face.

But Clint didn't need to see the man's face to recognize the figure as the same one who'd attacked him in the laundry. Those quick steps and stooped posture were unmistakable.

"Gotcha," Clint muttered as he slowly turned to get a little closer before starting the chase in earnest.

Since he was still a ways off, Clint kept the slender figure in the corner of his eye while working his way slowly along the deck. Once the people from the shore were making their way onto the boat, Clint used them for a bit of cover and headed toward the other end. When he wove through the new arrivals, there wasn't a trace of the slender man who'd been there before.

Clint picked up his pace and made it to the spot where he'd seen the man. His hand was on his gun, but there wasn't a target in sight. Just because he couldn't see the other man, Clint didn't relax for a second. He quickly turned his back to the rail, so nobody could sneak up behind him, and continued searching for the route the other man had used to get away.

There were a few doors close to the spot, but the longer Clint thought about it, the more possibilities he came up with. Since choosing any one of them would be nothing more than a shot in the dark, Clint cursed under his breath and walked away.

The new passengers were on the deck and shaking hands with a few men in nice suits. The gangplank was already being hauled back onto the boat, and the hands were pulling in the ropes that tied the *Misty Morning* to the little dock. Clint was about to head back down the stairs when he saw another familiar, slender figure walking along the rail.

Mia stood in roughly the same spot where Clint had been while the riverboat approached the dock. She wrapped her arms around herself and rubbed them to keep warm in the cool night air. When she saw him, Mia smiled at Clint and waited for him to come to her.

"Looks like they weren't after food after all," Clint said as he approached her. "Just a few more passengers."

"They got food, as well," she replied. "I watched them carry on some barrels and boxes while you were busy running along the deck."

"Oh. I guess I got a little distracted."

"You mind telling me what distracted you? I might be able to use that when the stakes get higher."

Clint laughed and shook his head. "Not on your life. You're already a big enough threat to my bankroll."

"All right, then," Mia said as she ran her fingers along Clint's lapel. "Then perhaps you could explain this suit. When you first walked in wearing it, you looked like something was wrong."

"It may be just some bad luck, but I did stumble into a situation." Without spelling out every last detail of what had happened, Clint told Mia about his scuffle in the laundry. She listened carefully and wound up pulling in a quick breath when he told her about the man's aptitude with a knife.

"Good God," she said. "And you just came back up to play cards after all that?"

"I couldn't find him on my own. I told the men who guard the doors, so there really wasn't much else for me to do. He's probably just some thief out to steal someone's winnings."

"Or he could be something a lot worse," Mia pointed out. "He could have killed you, Clint."

Shrugging, Clint said, "I've seen worse fights in saloons over much less money than what's being thrown around here. Even with guns being taken before cards are dealt, there could be more trouble than some lunatic hiding in a pile of dirty clothes."

"Do you remember what he looked like?"

"Sure. He was skinny. Moved like a snake and was damn good with a blade."

"Did he talk funny?"

Clint was about to answer that right away, but he paused as something came to mind. "Come to think of it, he might have had an accent. It may have been a British accent, but it sounded a lot sloppier than other Englishmen I've heard. How did you know about that?"

"I didn't," Mia replied. "I'm just trying to think of some way you could narrow it down. Maybe if we ask around, someone can help us find him."

Even though Clint hadn't played very much poker with her, he thought he caught the faint scent of a bluff coming from Mia just then. Deciding not to call her on it, he let it pass and headed down to the laundry to check on his suit.

TWENTY-ONE

The door to the laundry was locked. Since there was barely a soul in the hallways anywhere near that room, Clint honestly didn't expect anything else. And he didn't expect one of the doors clear down at the other end of the hall to pop open after he'd only rattled the laundry's door a few times.

It was the Chinese lady who popped her head out, and she smiled widely when she saw who was making the little bit of noise. "I'm glad it is you," she exclaimed. "Stay there. I fixed your suit."

Clint took a few steps toward her door, but didn't even make it halfway before she stepped out again. The lady had Clint's suit draped over her arm as if it was a royal cloak.

"I stitched it up as best I could," she said. "I cleaned, too, but it wasn't that dirty. Just wrinkled." When she saw Clint hold the suit and look at it, she asked, "Is it all right?"

"It's better than all right," he told her. "Honestly, I was just hoping to get my own clothes back. This loaner doesn't exactly suit me."

"Come in here and try it on," she said. "If I missed something, I can fix before you go."

"No, that's all right. I'll just take—"

"Come in here now!" she snapped.

82

Before Clint could get another word out, he found himself running toward the Chinese woman like a kid being threatened with a freshly cut switch. Her room was small, but meticulously clean. Tapping a stool with one hand, she quickly gathered up a needle and thread.

Clint shed the suit jacket and put his own on in its place. The Chinese woman looked over every last inch and then wound up smiling in front of him.

"Good as new," she said.

"How much do I owe you?"

"I owe you my life," she replied. "Fixing your suit is the least I can do. Don't insult me by offering money, too."

"All right. Thanks so much." After stepping down from the stool, Clint said, "There is one more thing."

Her eyes widened expectantly, but she waited quietly for Clint to continue.

"Has that man with the knife been around here any more?"

She shook her head. "No, but I think I might know what room he's in."

Clint stood there for a moment to figure out if he'd heard her correctly. Although the lady spoke with a slight accent, there wasn't enough of one to make her hard to understand.

"How would you know that?" he asked.

She walked to her door and motioned for him to follow. Using a key she took from her pocket, she led him into the laundry and turned the knob on the only lamp in the room. That lamp didn't produce very much light, but she maneuvered around the piles of clothes and stacks of baskets as if she could have done so in her sleep.

"Look," she said as she took a hanger from one of the hooks on the wall. "See?"

All Clint saw was a set of clothes on a hanger. Looking a bit closer, he picked out a red stain on the collar of the shirt. "Is that blood?" he asked.

She nodded. "Blood on a shirt that man with the knife was wearing. You hit him in the face, remember?"

Clint remembered, but he didn't recall seeing the man bleed. He sure as hell didn't remember if some blood had dripped onto his collar. "This could have come from someone else," he pointed out. "How are you so sure it's his?"

"This one has cream-colored buttons and not black. It has a shorter collar and these sleeves were rolled up just as far as the ones on that man's shirt when he was down here swinging that knife around. I wouldn't forget anything about that crazy man."

The longer he stared at that shirt, the less Clint seemed to recall what that man had been wearing. He remembered the knife in his hand and the way he'd fought. The rest just hadn't seemed all that important.

It was obvious that the Chinese woman wasn't lying to him. She spoke with as much conviction as a preacher quoting the scripture. Clint supposed that made sense since she was talking about things she saw and worked with every day. If someone needed to know about a model of a gun or how to modify a rifle's sights, they would probably get a similar earful from Clint.

"All right," he said. "Suppose that is his shirt."

"It is! And look," she said while holding the hanger a little closer to Clint. "There's the room it came from."

There was a tag pinned to the shirt with the number five written on it. "Is there a way for me to get into that room and have a look?" Clint asked.

"I don't have a key, but I can get one from the maid. She's sleeping now, but I could go wake her up."

"If it wouldn't be too much trouble."

The Chinese lady nodded and hurried out of the room. Before Clint could finish going through the pockets of the bloody shirt and put it back on its hook, the lady returned.

"I didn't even have to wake her," the lady explained. "Her spare key was on a hook where I keep mine. You can keep it for as long as you want. If she needs it, I'll say I took it and I'll come find you."

"I appreciate this," Clint said. "I'll try to get this back to you as soon as I can."

"Just try to catch that crazy man. If you need anything else, you just ask for Lucy."

"Lucy?"

She rolled her eyes and shook her head. "It's just what everyone calls me. You won't get nowhere if you ask for me by my real name."

Clint tipped his hat and left. Now that the riverboat was moving again, the poker games should be back in full swing. Just to be safe, Clint decided to change clothes and wait awhile before paying a visit to room number five. On a boat full of gamblers, the odds of finding an empty room would only increase as the night moved along.

TWENTY-TWO

By the time Clint made it back to his room, he was itching to get out of the borrowed suit and into a familiar set of clothes. That itch became even greater when he opened his door and got a look at what was waiting for him inside. Seeing Gretchen lying on his bed with nothing but a sheet draped over her made Clint forget all about getting into his own freshly stitched suit.

"What are you doing here?" Clint asked in surprise.

Gretchen stretched her arms over her head and arched her back. Those motions dropped the sheet almost all the way off of her body. The only reason it didn't fall completely off of her was because it hung on her breasts just long enough for her to get ahold of it again.

"If you object to me being here," she said, "I could just leave."

Clint stepped into the small cabin and closed the door behind him. Like most of the other cabins on the *Misty Morning*, his was just big enough to hold a cot, a trunk and a stool. Simply stepping all the way inside to let the door close was enough to put Clint close enough to smell the sweet scent of Gretchen's skin.

"You don't have to leave," Clint explained. "You just

86

caught me off guard. How'd you know which room was mine?"

She sat up so her back was against the wall, one leg was curled beneath her and the other dangled off the side of the cot. She used both hands to hold the sheet over her breasts, but let enough of her show to make it obvious she wasn't wearing a stitch of clothing underneath. "I asked one of the crew."

Although that wasn't much of an explanation, Clint didn't need to hear much more to imagine her powers of persuasion. In fact, he was feeling some of those powers at that very moment.

"I hoped you'd be heading back here," she told him. "Since you probably wouldn't be leaving the tables too much later on, I wanted to get ahold of you when I had the chance."

Gretchen repositioned herself so she was on her knees on the bed. She dropped the sheet and leaned forward so she could pull Clint closer to her. "I love being on boats," she whispered. "We're always moving, and it makes me want to grab hold of someone and move some more. I knew you were that someone the moment I felt your hands on me."

Clint tried to think of when he'd had a chance to put his hands on her. Rather than waste time with that, however, he took the opportunity that was right in front of him and placed his hands on the smooth contours of her sides and hips.

Pressing herself even closer against him, Gretchen nuzzled her face against Clint's neck and all but purred when she felt his fingers glide along the gentle slope of her back. She then began pulling off his suit, and was so quick to get his pants off that she ripped one of the seams.

"Sorry about that," she said.

Clint laughed and ripped the pants some more as he kicked them off. "Don't worry about it. I borrowed the suit."

The sound of the fabric ripping seemed to light a fire inside of Gretchen, because she sat on the edge of the cot and wrapped her lips around Clint's cock as if she was starving for the taste of him. Her mouth tightened around him, and she took every inch of him in while her tongue circled his thick column of flesh faster and faster.

Clint braced himself against the wall as Gretchen sucked him vigorously. Soon, he pulled her head back and pushed her onto the cot so he could climb on top of her. He was right in thinking that would excite her even more, because Gretchen let out a pleasured gasp when her back hit the cot. She spread her legs open wide and squirmed anxiously as he settled on top of her.

The cot was just wide enough to sleep one person comfortably, so two people putting it to use was something else entirely. After a few quick trials, Clint realized he would have a problem if he continued along this same path. Since stopping wasn't an option, he pushed the cot away from the wall so he could straddle both it and Gretchen.

The hair between her legs was the same golden shade as the long strands from the top of her head. It felt wet and soft as Clint plunged his cock into her. Gretchen let out a throaty moan as she reached back to grab hold of the cot on either side of her head. Every time Clint thrust into her, she pumped her hips forward.

Pretty soon, Clint had to tighten his grip on the cot to keep it from moving around too much. He found it was easier to grab hold of Gretchen instead. Actually, that way turned out to be a whole lot more fun as well.

Her backside was plump and soft in his hands. Clint lifted her just a bit off the cot so he could thrust between her legs without pushing the cot against the wall. With her still grabbing onto the other end of the cot, they struck a perfect balance that allowed Clint to pound into her again and again, while Gretchen arched her back and let her orgasm pump through her.

When her climax was over, Gretchen's body went limp. Clint set her onto the cot and stood over her to catch his breath. She lay with her hair flowing to one side and sweat glistening between her breasts. That sight was more than enough to give Clint the energy he needed to straddle her once more.

Rather than hold her up, he lifted her legs so they were lying upward against his chest. He slid into her easily from that angle and drove all the way inside. Gretchen moaned softly as Clint slipped in and out of her. When she looked up at him, it was with an exhausted smile. She pulled her legs back until her knees were close to her chest. That way, Clint could settle on top of her a bit more and enter her from a slightly better angle.

Clint knew he was hitting a sweet spot inside of her because he could feel Gretchen's entire body tremble. Running his hands along the gentle curves of her backside, Clint buried his cock deep inside of her. When he pulled out, he allowed himself to slip completely out of her and then slid right back in again.

A few more of those, and Gretchen was breathing heavily as another orgasm built up. This time, when she let out a long, pleasured moan, Clint did the same. He drove all the way inside of her and pushed just a little deeper, until his own climax made him weak in the knees.

TWENTY-THREE

Clint was up a hundred dollars and could have been up even more if he hadn't been trying so hard to lose. The main room was full of new faces, but most of the ones at his table were familiar. Jones and Barry were still there. Mia sat in her normal seat and, every so often, someone else would drift in and out of the game.

The only time anyone asked any questions was when someone got up to leave the game. When that happened, people looked at the deserter with confusion and pure shock. The night was still young and they were all there to gamble. If not, then more than a few people would ask what else better there was to do on that boat.

Gretchen wasn't anywhere to be seen after Clint left his room, so that excuse wasn't available.

He didn't want to risk being spotted walking in the wrong direction if he simply said he had to relieve himself by getting rid of some of the beer he'd been drinking. That only left one more reason why a gambler would volunteer to walk away from one of the best poker games around.

Clint had to lose.

At first, it seemed like a fairly easy thing to do. He

didn't want to be too obvious about it, because that could draw as much suspicion as cheating to win. He also didn't want to lose too much because he still planned on playing some cards when he was done sorting through his other business.

Unfortunately, Lady Luck still wasn't done smiling on him after the gift Clint had gotten in his room earlier that night. Even though he meant to lose a chunk of his winnings for the sake of getting some time away from the poker room, Clint couldn't possibly throw away some of the hands he was dealt.

Tossing a natural flush was the same as asking him to toss a pet over the side of a cliff.

Pitching the straight flush he'd filled in after drawing one card would have been harder than cutting off his own arm.

Finally, Clint swallowed his gambling instincts and folded after glancing toward his cards without actually looking at them. "I need to get some fresh air," he said.

"What?" Barry asked. "Why?"

"I just want to get up and stretch my legs."

"What's the matter?"

"Nothing."

"Maybe I'll come with you. I got a few things I'd like to discuss."

Clint had no clue what could be on Barry's mind, but he didn't want to find out. Before he was roped into an entire conversation about it, he waved the man off and waited for his next hand to be dealt. This time, he smirked and only asked for one card after raising the bet. When he got his card, Clint raised again.

"I think I got you now," Barry said.

"Can you beat a flush?" Clint asked.

"Aw shit."

Clint laid down his cards and started to reach for the chips. Before he could touch one of them, his hand was grabbed by a cold, iron grip.

"Not so fast," Jones snapped as he pulled Clint's hand away from the pot. "That's not a flush."

"What are you talking about? That's a ten-high club flush."

"That ten isn't a club. It's a spade."

Clint squinted down at the cards and then glared up at Barry. "You see what happened? I wanted to stretch my legs, you made me stay and now look!"

Barry winced and gave a halfhearted shrug.

"You mind if I get up and take my stretch now?" Clint snarled.

"Nope," Barry replied.

"Alone?"

"Be my guest."

Clint walked out of the room looking every bit as frustrated as he felt. It seemed that winning as much as he did had had its disadvantages after all. The players either wanted to get their money back or keep their eye on him to make sure he wasn't cheating. Either way, they sure as hell didn't want to let him go. After Clint's display, however, the table was more than willing to give him some time to himself.

The moment he stepped outside into the night air, Clint felt better. The cool breeze felt like a splash of water on his face, and the sounds of the river were a welcome relief from the noise that filled the inside of the *Misty Morning*'s poker room.

Since there wasn't anyone else wandering the deck, Clint made a straight line for the door that led down into the section where the sleeping cabins were located. As soon as he got to the bottom of the stairs, Clint could tell he wasn't going to be alone in the hallway. A few voices drifted to his ears, and stopped at the sound of Clint's first step.

It was too late to think he might get in without being noticed.

In fact, the longer the voices stayed quiet, the more uncomfortable Clint felt.

When he heard the first steps heading toward the stairs, Clint felt completely exposed.

The top of the stairs wasn't lit, so Clint was standing in the middle of thick shadows. The door behind him was closed, and he kept it that way by holding one hand on the knob. Just before he caught sight of feet in the hallway at the base of the narrow staircase, Clint threw open the door and stomped outside.

As soon as he was clear of the stairs, Clint eased up on his footing so his boots didn't slam so hard against the deck. There was a door leading into the riverboat's dining area and saloon, which was on the same level as the deck he was on. Clint entered the saloon and hurried toward the thickest cluster of people he could find.

Behind him, Clint heard the saloon door open again. He didn't even glance over his shoulder. Instead, Clint kept a casual smile on his face as he brushed past several gamblers trying to talk to some very attractive ladies, and kept moving toward the door at the opposite end of the room. It was only a matter of seconds before Clint reached it, but he felt as if he'd run a mile to get there.

Clint eased that door open just enough for him to slip through. Once outside, he ran around the corner to wind up at the door leading back down to the private cabins. There was a man wearing a gun belt standing with his back to Clint, looking around the first corner that Clint had turned to get to the saloon. Now that he'd gotten around and behind that man, Clint moved quickly and quietly to the smaller door leading to the first hallway.

Walking down those same stairs this time around, Clint's head was spinning. He'd basically run in a wide circle, but had gone through so many doors that they all seemed to blend together. This time, there were no voices in the hallway. Clint couldn't see very far past the bottom of the steep stairs, so he headed down them prepared for anything.

There was one man standing at the door marked by a number five. He was already looking toward the stairs with his hand on his holstered gun.

Before the armed man could say anything, Clint anxiously asked, "Are you the one who might be able to help those other two?"

"What other two?"

"The ones who just ran up those stairs. They told me to tell the other one to get up there and help them with—"

Clint didn't even need to finish his lie before the gunman bolted past him and charged up the stairs. Not wanting to waste a second of the time he'd bought for himself, Clint took the maid's key from his pocket and unlocked the door to room number five.

TWENTY-FOUR

The room actually wasn't much bigger than Clint's. Although the cot appeared to be a bit more comfortable, the only other difference was the table situated against one wall. Clint headed over to that table and took a look at the solitaire layout that was there.

He didn't know exactly what he was looking for, so Clint just started rummaging. Part of him felt a little bad about going through someone else's things, especially since he wasn't completely sure they belonged to the man he was after. Since it didn't seem like there was going to be much to find anyway, Clint sifted through what was there and hoped for the best.

Unfortunately, his luck wasn't holding up there as well as it had been in the poker room. There was no knife lying out for him to find, another bloody piece of clothing or anything else that might possibly be of any help. Even if the things he found did belong to the man with the knife, none of them would do him any good.

That's when Clint stopped and reminded himself of what he was after in the first place. He needed something to tell him why someone would go to such lengths to stow away aboard the *Misty Morning*, where they might have gone once they were on board, and who that person might be. If he found something to tie the man to attacking Clint, that would be even better.

Clint's heart pounded faster and faster as if he could feel the gunmen coming back from being distracted. He had even less time available if he wanted to walk out of that room rather than fight his way out. With no better ideas coming to him, Clint dropped to his hands and knees to get a closer look at the floor.

As he shuffled toward the cot, Clint's right hand slapped against a flat piece of paper mostly hidden beneath the bed. At first, he thought it was an invitation similar to the one he'd gotten. His hopes soared, since an invitation like his would have a name on it.

The envelope turned out to be the wrong size to contain an invitation. It was also empty. There was, however, some writing in one corner of the back of the envelope. Clint held it closer so he could read the scribbled letters in the room's dim light: DCRM1—that was all that was written on the envelope. Since there wasn't anything else there and the floor was otherwise clean, Clint got up and started walking toward the door. He stopped when he spotted something on the table that caught his attention. Along with the cards spread out in a solitaire game layout, there were other decks of cards on the edge of the table. But what had caught Clint's eye wasn't the cards. The glint of metal coming from beneath one of the decks interested him even more.

Lifting that deck, Clint recognized the small tool beneath it as a set of shears used to trim the edges of cards so the dealer could manipulate who got what. If there were shears in the room, that meant the person in that room was a card cheat. It also meant the odds were very good that trimming edges of cards wasn't that person's only method of getting his results.

Clint picked up the deck and examined the backs of the cards. For the most part, they bore standard patterns that could be found on any cards. Since he had some idea of what to look for, Clint soon picked out a few marks here and there that didn't belong.

Whoever had marked the cards was smart. The marks were difficult to spot and might have gone unnoticed if Clint wasn't certain they'd be there. Even though he did spot them, the marks weren't in any particular pattern to make them easy to read. That was a trick used by more sophisticated cheats, since they had to memorize an entire alphabet of code rather than a simple pattern of marks in certain spots telling number or suit.

Even marks within suits were different, which would have made the deck more trouble than it was worth to most cheats. This one, however, didn't mind memorizing fifty-two disconnected markings. It also meant he had to be awfully good at substituting his deck in the middle of a game. As Clint was about to put the cards back where he'd found them, he realized something else: The marks on the back were exactly like the ones used in the *Misty Morning*'s poker room.

Not close.

Not very close.

Exactly the same.

And since those cards were using a fairly distinctive pattern, that meant whoever had marked those cards had somehow gotten enough time to do so after boarding, or already knew what that pattern would be.

All of these bits of information settled into Clint's head as he straightened up and covered any signs that he'd been there. They weren't exactly the definitive clues he'd been hoping for, but he certainly knew a lot more now than when he'd come in.

There was still plenty more that he didn't know, but that would have to remain a mystery for the time being. What concerned Clint more was getting out of that room before he was either discovered or trapped in by all those armed men.

Taking a quick look under the door, Clint didn't see any feet on the other side. He opened the door, took another quick look, and then stepped into the hall.

That one step brought his heart right to the top of his throat. If someone was waiting out there for him, they would have a possibly fatal advantage. Even if there was someone close to the upstairs door, they would see Clint leaving the room with more than enough time to do something about it.

Clint was just quick enough to avoid a fight and heard the door at the top of the stairs swinging open as soon as he pulled the room's door shut behind him. He dashed down the hall and turned the first corner he found. Behind him, Clint could hear heavy steps as the gunmen took their positions by the room door and talked about who'd been the one to lose sight of Clint in the saloon.

"Is there a problem, sir?"

Clint twitched at the sound of the voice, but recognized it. He turned around and realized he was standing in the entrance to what appeared to be a small kitchen. Filling up most of the doorway leading to the kitchen, Arvin waited for an answer to his question.

"Hello, Arvin," Clint said.

"Hello. Is there a problem?"

"Yeah. I'm a bit lost."

"That depends on where you're trying to go."

"I'd like to get back to the poker room, but I'd rather not head down that hallway again. Some of those men with the guns followed me into the saloon like they were going to steal my money."

Arvin's brow furrowed and he slowly shook his head. "I highly doubt that, sir."

"Well, if it's all the same to you, I'd appreciate another way up. I kind of already made some accusations and they didn't take it too kindly."

"Ah. I see. This kitchen serves food to these rooms as well as the saloon. I hope you don't mind showing your face there again, because that's your only alternative."

"Thanks, Arvin," Clint said as he followed the man with the salt-and-pepper hair. "You pulled my fat from the fire again."

"That's . . . nice, sir."

TWENTY-FIVE

When Clint got back to the main poker room, he noticed a slight difference at the tables. They were still mostly full, but very few of them seemed familiar. Granted, Clint hadn't memorized every last face, but he'd been sitting there long enough to get a feel for the tables around him. Now that he got closer, he realized even his table wasn't the same.

Elsa was the only one in her original spot, and she'd attracted a fresh batch of admirers. When she saw Clint approaching the table, she gave a few quick farewells and got up to meet Clint before he got there.

"Where did everyone go?" Clint asked.

"All the big games have moved to the smaller rooms," she replied.

"I guess that's not a big surprise."

"No, but you might want to consider staying in here anyway," Elsa told him with a crafty smirk.

"Why?"

"Because these new players are either too rich to care about losing a few hands or too stupid to know how to avoid it."

"I appreciate the thought, but I think I'd rather up my game instead of wringing someone else dry."

"Isn't wringing the other players dry the point of poker?"

Clint paused for a second and then shrugged. "I guess so, but it's more fun to play for higher stakes. Besides, I was getting used to the game we'd already started."

Elsa smiled and slipped her arm around Clint's. Although the move was similar to the way Gretchen had attached herself to him, Elsa moved in a completely different way than her sister. Where Gretchen had practically drifted next to Clint, Elsa led him in the exact direction she wanted him to go.

"Bigger stakes, huh?" Elsa said. "I like the way you think."

"You're not staying? It looks like there's a bunch of fellows who'll be very disappointed about that."

She waved and turned her back on the table as if it no longer existed. "They can find me if they want, but I'd rather play for higher stakes, too. I was actually just trying to get you to stay so you wouldn't be the one to rob me blind tonight."

"I'm not that good of a player," Clint said.

Laughing as she pushed open the door leading toward the back of the boat, Elsa said, "I'd consider letting you do plenty of things to me, Clint Adams. Treating me like an idiot isn't one of them."

"All right, then," Clint said. "Then maybe we could go over some of the things you would let me do."

When Elsa looked at him, she recognized the flirtatious look in his eye and shot back a look of her own that was enough to send a warm shiver under Clint's skin. "Later," she said without one bit of doubt in her voice. "For now, I'm just supposed to take you to this game and be quick about it. The others are saving you a seat, but I'm not sure how much longer Jones will hold out."

"Probably until his luck turns."

"Good point. By the way, do you know a man named Vessele?"

"Vessele?" Clint repeated as he let the name drift through his mind. Before long, he nodded. "Jean Claude Vessele. I saw him on the dock when I was waiting to board."

"He was asking about you. Seems like he wants in on our game."

"He's welcome to sit in at the poker table." Pulling Elsa a little closer, Clint added, "The other games I have in mind will just be between you and me."

"I'll be sure to let Gretchen know about that," Elsa replied. She kept her expression rock solid for the entire rest of the walk to the back poker room. Once there, she let Clint see enough of a grin to let him know that he was off the hook. "They're waiting for you over there."

Elsa didn't really need to say anything or even point out which table she meant. The room was so much smaller than the first one that Clint could see practically everything in it with one glance.

Compared to the main poker room, this one was a glorified closet. To be fair, however, it looked closer to something one might expect on a riverboat. There were no rugs on the floor. There were only a few decorations hanging here and there, with plenty of round portholes lining the walls.

The room was lit by a few lanterns hanging from the roof, which all swayed to the motions of the river as the *Misty Morning* churned through the water. Those lanterns hung low enough for Clint to watch his step and occasionally duck as he made his way to the table in the back. That part of the room felt even more cramped than the rest, since the wall and roof were slanted to make space for the paddle wheel. That large machinery on the other side of the wall also managed to fill the room with a loud, constant rumble.

"Howdy!" Barry shouted as soon as he saw Clint headed toward the table.

Apart from Barry, only Jones was sitting there waiting for them.

Clint grinned and sat down at one of the several empty chairs. "Where's Mia?" he asked.

"She should be back in a while," Jones replied.

Barry chuckled and took a sip of his whiskey. "Went to powder her nose. You hear that Jean Claude Vessele was askin' for ya?"

"I sure did. Where is he?"

Barry glanced around and then shrugged. "Beats me. Nobody's seen him since he came around askin' about you. He's probably found himself another tree to prune."

Even though Clint didn't like the sound of that, he also didn't like the thought of poking around the boat so soon after getting away from those armed men guarding room number five. His mind was made up as several other gamblers came and went from the room in the short time it took for Clint to get settled.

"To hell with 'em," Barry grunted. "Four's enough for a game. Or are you tired, Adams?"

"Shut up and deal."

"Now that's what I like to hear!"

TWENTY-SIX

Jean Claude's silk suit was drenched with sweat.

His banded collar shirt was stained with blood.

His arms were tied behind his back, and his head lolled forward as if it was only loosely connected to his neck.

"You think I forgot about you?" Dench asked as he circled Jean Claude's chair like a vulture.

Jean Claude lifted his head and took a moment to get his eyes to focus. When he was able to look at Dench directly, he replied, "I wouldn't think you'd forget about me. Not after that beating I gave you in Denison."

Nodding slowly, Dench started to turn his back on Jean Claude. Then he quickly spun back around and sent his fist directly into Jean Claude's face. His knuckles impacted with a wet crack that snapped Jean Claude's head back and sent some blood through the air.

"How'd you like that?" Dench rasped in a guttural English accent.

"Since that seemed like the best you could do," Jean Claude replied, "I like it just fine."

Dench kept his eyes level with Jean Claude's as he reached to his belt and wrapped his fingers around the handle of the knife kept there. When he took the knife from its scabbard, he did it as if he was savoring every last moment. By the time the entire blade was out, Dench was wide-eyed and smiling anxiously. "I can do a whole lot better," he said. "You just wait and see."

The room where Jean Claude was being held was long and narrow. The walls were made of thick wood nailed together so tightly that the boards creaked every time the riverboat listed more than an inch in any direction. The air was stagnant and smelled like dried blood, which seemed chilling when the hooks dangling from the roof clanged together.

"I'd consider changing my tune if I were you," Solomon said as he stepped forward so Jean Claude could see him better. "Dench here could slice you open and let you bleed for days. Seeing as how fresh meat is usually kept here, I doubt anyone will notice."

"Someone will find me," Jean Claude said.

"I doubt that very much. The *Misty Morning* won't be on the river that long. Besides, gamblers don't generally eat at all during events like this. I doubt they'll be demanding steaks or pork chops."

"That's not what I meant. I'm expected at games. Plenty of folks know I'm here."

Coming to a stop behind Jean Claude's chair, Solomon grabbed a fistful of the man's hair and jerked his head back. "I know you're here. That's all you should care about right now."

"What do you want from me?" Jean Claude asked.

Solomon walked back around so Jean Claude could see him. "Your bankroll, for starters."

"Take it. I can always win more."

"If you mean you can get more from your rich grandparents, I doubt that very much. You see, a good portion of that money will be handed over to ensure your safe return."

"My grandparents haven't spoken to me in—"

Jean Claude was cut off by a quick slash from Dench's

blade. The razor-sharp edge glanced across his chest, but that was enough to slice through his shirt and open a shallow wound. Blood trickled out, which caused Dench's eyes to widen.

"You think you're so bloody smart?" Dench grunted. "You cheated me in Denison. Well, now I'm about to get my money back."

"You can have double if you cut me loose and turn that blade on the dandy standing over there."

Dench glanced over to Solomon as if he was checking to see if there were any other well-dressed men standing in the meat compartment. When he looked back, Dench was laughing to himself. "After the grief you caused me, there's not a price you can pay for me to set you free. Besides, I'll be making back more than double what you took."

"You'll set me free soon enough once my ransom is paid," Jean Claude said. "Otherwise, you'll have more bounty hunters than you knew existed coming after you."

Dench's blade came down in a swift arc that flickered like a passing thought. After embedding the blade into the arm of the chair, Dench reached out with his other hand to catch the finger that fell from Jean Claude's hand.

"Maybe not all of you will get set free," Dench said as he waved the finger at the man who'd grown it.

TWENTY-SEVEN

Clint woke up in his cabin without remembering exactly how he'd gotten there. He'd had his share of beer during the night, but he hadn't passed out drunk. Instead, it was the night itself that had done him in. To be more precise, it was the night that dragged until morning without a wink of sleep in between.

Even though sunlight blazed through the little porthole to illuminate his cramped cabin, Clint had to think what time of day it was. He couldn't even narrow it down to morning or afternoon. Instead, he had to dig for his watch and check it for himself.

"Jesus," he muttered when he saw that it was actually after noon and not merely close to it.

Going through the motions of pulling on his clothes after swinging his feet over the side of his cot, Clint quickly realized that he was still wearing his suit from the night before. He pulled that off, folded it neatly and put on his jeans and a plain shirt. That wasn't enough to make him feel like a human being just yet, so Clint struck out in search of some coffee.

He found it in the saloon on the upper deck, which was the same place that had allowed him to make an escape from room number five. Clint walked into the saloon, only to find a good number of familiar faces in there already. Most of those faces appeared to be as out of sorts as he was.

"Mornin'," the bartender said in a chipper tone that must have taxed more than a few nerves. "You look like you need some coffee."

"Popular request, huh?" Clint asked.

"At least amongst you sporting fellas." The bartender turned around and picked up a steaming kettle. After filling a cup with dark brew, he set it in front of Clint's spot at the bar and asked, "How'd you make out last night?"

"Not too bad."

"Well, there's games going all day and night, so jump back in as soon as you feel inclined."

"Is Arvin around?"

The bartender paused for a moment, but only because he seemed to be somewhat taken aback by the question. After a few blinks, he replied, "Sure. He's always wandering around this boat somewhere."

"Any idea where I might find him?"

"He'll be in the dining room during the meals and around the poker room later at night. If it's too late, he'll be asleep, but other than that, he could be anywhere. Why do you ask?"

"Just checking. What else have you got besides the coffee?"

"They should still be serving something in the dining room. We don't have much here besides a few eggs and maybe some toast."

"That'd be perfect," Clint said. "You think you could scrape some of that up for me?"

"Sure. I'll see what I can do."

Clint sipped his coffee and turned around so he could lean against the bar while looking out the windows. It was a bright day, and he could see a little bit of the river as well as a sample of the shore. As he waited, Clint saw a large house drift into view. By the time it drifted away again, the bartender had reappeared from the small stairs that Clint had used the night before. He had a plate piled high with scrambled eggs and a few slices of toast.

"Here you go," the bartender said.

Clint rubbed his hands together and grinned. Just smelling the breakfast was enough to remind him of how hungry he was. "Perfect. How much?"

"Forget about it."

"What?"

The bartender waved at Clint and refilled his coffee. "You missed out on most of what they were serving, and this is just some of the leftovers. I couldn't charge you for that."

"Well, I appreciate it." Digging into his pocket, Clint took out enough money to cover what that food should have cost. "For the coffee," he said. "Keep the change."

The bartender nodded, tucked the money away and continued with what he'd been doing before Clint had arrived.

Clint ate his eggs and savored the quiet of the saloon. Since most of the gamblers had stayed up just as late, or later, than he had, they were still just as tired. The ones who'd drank more were nursing either headaches or a whiskey in one of the saloon's darker corners. Either way, none of them were feeling as boisterous as they had been the previous night.

Although Clint was certain the poker rooms were still just as lively as ever, he figured on giving himself some peace and quiet for at least as much time as it took for him to eat his breakfast and let the food settle. Unless trouble came to find him, he guessed his little plan shouldn't be too hard to carry out.

Right on cue, Mia ran past the saloon like she'd been tossed past the windows. She came right back and glared through one window to fix her eyes upon Clint. As soon as she found the door, she rushed straight to him.

"There you are, Clint," she said breathlessly. "I've been looking all over for you."

"Well," Clint said regretfully, "here I am."

"Did you know Jean Claude Vessele was looking for you?"

"Yeah, but he never showed up. Come to think of it," Clint added, "you disappeared last night, too."

"I'm here now, but Vessele is still missing."

Clint straightened up and asked, "Missing?"

She nodded. "And he's not the only one."

TWENTY-EIGHT

Mia fluttered around the saloon like a nervous humming-bird while Clint downed his coffee and piled some eggs between two slices of toast. It took him all of half a minute to do that, but she fretted as if he was taking his own sweet time.

Clint was actually anxious, too, but he figured he might not be able to stop and eat if things went to hell. Hopefully, that wouldn't be quite the case.

"All right," he said once they were outside the saloon. "Tell me what happened."

"I've been looking for Jean Claude and he's nowhere to be found."

"Maybe he's in his room."

"I checked there," she replied almost instantly.

"Then maybe he's in someone else's room. Mia, this isn't exactly the sort of thing where a man feels like he's got to check in every few minutes. This is a riverboat full of poker games and pretty women. It's kind of easy to get lost in something like that."

Although she was still anxious, Mia shifted her eyes to him and said, "I suppose you'd know all about that."

"Yeah," Clint said without hesitation. "I sure would. I'm not here to work, you know."

Mia grabbed Clint by the elbow and pulled him even farther away from the saloon. Before she started talking, she spotted a pair of men walking toward them and then pulled Clint even closer to the rail. Once those men had walked by, she whispered, "I *am* here to work."

"What do you mean?"

"There's some men on board this boat who are wanted by the law, and I mean to bring them in before they do any damage. At least, I'd hoped to get to them in time, but it looks like I'm already too late."

Clint chewed on the eggs and toast he'd bitten off and then swallowed. "So you're a bounty hunter?"

Mia shook her head and looked around some more. Since there wasn't anyone in earshot apart from a few birds circling overhead, she told him, "I work with the Texas Rangers." When she saw the look that brought to Clint's face, she asked, "What's so funny?"

"Nothing funny, just a little . . ."

"What?"

"Far-fetched is more like it." Clint wiped his mouth with the back of his hand so he could speak a little clearer. "I've worked with plenty of Texas Rangers and they're a proud bunch. They're also not the sort who would allow a woman to ride along with them. No offense, but that's just the way they are."

"So you think I'm lying?"

"Not yet. Keep talking."

Sighing, Mia continued in a strained voice. "Do you know of a man named Jack Solomon?"

Clint thought that over as he took another bite of his sandwich. "No."

"He's wanted for everything under the sun, from stealing and running scams to kidnapping and murder. He's also very good at keeping his head down and not attracting a lot of attention. He arranged to get himself invited onto this riverboat so he could get a shot at all the rich gamblers coming on board."

"Then he's in for a surprise," Clint said. "I've never met a gambler who's truly rich."

"Have you met one that wouldn't scrape together one hell of a bankroll to prepare himself for something like this?"

Clint took another bite, but didn't have to think for very long to come up with the answer for that one. "Good point," he said through a mouthful of eggs.

"Lots of the gamblers here have some way to get their hands on more money if they need it badly enough," Mia continued. "Some have friends who owe them. Some have it stashed away in banks all over the country. And some, like Jean Claude Vessele, have rich families who can pull together plenty of cash if they had to."

"How do you know about Jean Claude's family?" Clint asked.

"We've been trying to get ahold of Jack Solomon for some time, and one of his killers led us to Vessele. That same killer led us to a bunch of other gamblers, until we found out they were all being scouted until they could all be brought to one place."

"So what's supposed to happen now that they're here?" Clint asked. "Is this Solomon fellow going to rob them right under the noses of all these armed guards?"

"I'm pretty sure at least some of those guards are working for Solomon. Considering his reputation and what we know about his partner, he might not need too many other men in order to snatch a few drunken gamblers. I think he's already got Jean Claude."

"And you're sure he's not passed out somewhere or sharing someone else's bed?"

Mia took hold of the railing and leaned forward so she could take a deep breath. "I searched this boat from top to bottom last night," she said. "I went everywhere Jean Claude would be able to go and asked anyone who might know where he was. I didn't find any trace of him and the people who know him were all just as worried as me."

Looking over to Clint, she asked, "Did you find that fellow with the knife? You remember . . . the one who talked funny."

Clint froze as he remembered the last time he'd talked to her regarding that matter. "No, I didn't find him," he said.

"Actually, he had an English accent, right?"

Clint nodded.

"And he was also about this tall, had sunken eyes and skin paler than a pig's belly. Am I close?"

"Not close," Clint said. "More like dead on the money."

TWENTY-NINE

"His name is Dench. I don't know if that's his first, middle, last or nickname, but that's what a few people call him. Most everyone else doesn't even know he's alive. He's killed dozens of men with that knife you saw and dozens more in ways you wouldn't even want to imagine. I've heard one man from Scotland Yard call him the Ripper, but that was more of a sick joke than a serious accusation."

Clint listened to her and felt a coldness work its way up his spine. Before he let the rest of his sandwich fall from his hands, he stuffed it into his mouth and quickly swallowed it down.

"You look pale," Mia said. "Is something wrong?"

"I thought you were working some sort of angle before. Now I'm not so sure."

"It's not an angle," she told him. "I do need your help, though. I was told you've helped the Rangers other times and have even saved some good men's lives."

"Who told you that?" Clint asked.

"The same Rangers who arranged to get that invitation mailed to you."

Clint let his head fall forward and muttered, "Jesus, are you telling me this whole thing was a setup to get me to

work with you? All you had to do was ask, not stage some
sort of show with you getting ambushed so I'd ride to the
rescue."

"That wasn't a show," Mia said. "I was hoping to meet
up with you at the dock and then I could introduce myself."

"Yeah? What about those men who attacked you? They
better not have been Rangers, because I sure as hell wasn't
firing pretend bullets at them!"

"Those were Solomon's men. I think they were checking up on me once they saw my name on the list to receive
an invitation."

"Nobody came to check on me," Clint pointed out.

"That's because anyone in Solomon's line of work, or
any gambler for that matter, would already know who you
are."

Clint wasn't about to blow his own horn, but he also
couldn't deny the point Mia had made.

She turned so she was leaning sideways against the rail
and looking Clint straight in the eyes. "If I was in your position, I would be suspicious, too. In fact, I was hoping to
get you to help me without having to tell you all of this."

"Why do that?"

"For the same reasons you mentioned before. Whenever
anyone thinks about the Texas Rangers, they picture big
men with big white hats charging out to bring in dangerous
killers." She laughed a bit and added, "Actually, that's really not too far from the truth. It's not easy being a woman
and working with them."

"So how'd you manage it?"

"In some ways . . . I didn't. A Ranger who knew I could
handle myself asked me to help him trap a wanted man in
Fort Griffin. Things worked out pretty good. I asked for a
job and he turned me down. He said it would be too hard
for me to be accepted into the Rangers and that other men
would be too concerned with watching out for me to get

their jobs done. That's why he only uses me to get in close when I can and work from the inside."

"Kind of like a spy," Clint pointed out.

After thinking that over, she shrugged and smiled. "I guess you could say that. Anyway, since Solomon was already checking up on the people on that list, we didn't want to risk coming to you and asking you directly to lend us a hand. If Solomon's men had caught sight of that, it could have made it a whole lot harder for us to catch him."

"All right, then," Clint said. "Everything you've been saying sounds fairly within reason. Then again, that says a lot if I consider all of this within reason."

Mia smirked. "I know what you mean."

"I've got two questions before I agree to help. First of all, that night we spent together on the way here . . . was that part of you trying to get close enough to me to sway me to your way of thinking?"

"No," Mia told him. "In fact, I could probably get into some serious trouble if certain members of the Rangers found out about that."

"Now for my second question. Who do you answer to in the Texas Rangers?"

"John Shaver."

"I've met him. How's Betty and the boys?"

Mia grinned again and replied, "His wife's name is Betsy, and he's only got one boy. He's also got one girl, and they're all doing fine."

Clint extended a hand for Mia to shake. "You've got yourself a partner."

THIRTY

Mia walked beside Clint as if they were merely out for a stroll around the boat. As they passed through a relatively empty hallway, she asked, "Tell me why we're looking for the porter?"

"Because he might be able to clear something up for me before I make a fool out of myself."

Before Mia could ask another question, Clint spotted Arvin moving from one room to another. He rushed toward the older man and got to him just before Arvin was out of sight.

"There you are," Clint said. "I've been looking for you."

"Excellent," the man replied dryly. "How can I be of service?"

"I'd like to pay a visit to a friend of mine, but I might have forgotten which room he's in. Could you tell me who's in room number five?"

Without hesitation, Arvin said, "That would be Mr. Randolph."

"I thought I was going to have to work a lot harder for that," Clint said.

"You would have if it had been any other room. That one is under guard and is quite disagreeable to the staff. A man like that likes drawing attention, so who am I to deny him? Is there anything else?"

"Nope. That'll do it."

Arvin was gone in the blink of an eye, allowing Clint and Mia to walk toward the end of the hall on their own.

"Does that name sound familiar?" Clint asked.

"Randolph is a name Solomon's used before. Is room number five his?"

"Yes, and I'm surprised you haven't found it already on your own."

"That's not the only room with armed men outside of it, you know. The last man to board was taken straight to a room of his own with plenty of firepower posted right outside of it."

"And here I can't even get into the poker room wearing a gun belt," Clint grumbled.

Mia shrugged and said, "It pays to bribe most of the men hired to provide security around here. I wouldn't be surprised if the captain of this boat on Solomon's payroll as well."

"Why wouldn't he be?" Clint asked. "It's not like he's got an actual rank or anything. All he needs to do is steer along a river and stop at a few docks along the way."

"Come to think of it, there doesn't even really have to be a captain."

"That's very true, so there's no reason for us to worry about him. The first thing I'd like to worry about is finding Jean Claude. Do you really think he's in this Solomon's sights?"

Mia nodded quickly. "I know he is. Vessele humiliated Dench at a poker game in Denison not too long ago. It was one of those losses that might make someone reconsider ever playing cards again. What made it worse is that Vessele bragged about it for weeks afterward."

"That's pretty odd considering Dench is supposed to be such a known killer."

"Jean Claude usually surrounds himself with friends or relatives that all carry guns."

"And none of them are on this boat?" Clint asked.

"None of them were invited."

Clint nodded slowly. "I'm starting to see why something like this would appeal to Solomon."

But Mia was walking faster and looking at Clint less and less. "Room number five isn't far away. We need to find a way to get in there," she said excitedly.

"I've already been in there."

"What?" Mia asked as her head snapped around. "When? How?"

"Last night and with this," Clint replied as he took the key from his pocket and showed it to her.

Mia stopped dead in her tracks and stared at the key as if she was trying to commit the curving shape to memory. Finally, she asked, "Was there anything in there worth seeing?"

"Not particularly. Just some marked cards and a note written on his copy of the invitation that said DCRM1."

"Are you sure that's what it said?"

Clint nodded. "After all the trouble I went through to get that little bit of nothing, I think I'd be able to remember it."

She stayed in her spot for a few seconds and then asked, "Why didn't you tell me this before?"

"Why didn't you tell me you were a Texas Ranger before?"

"I'm not a Texas Ranger."

"You know what I mean."

After conceding the point with a nod, Mia said, "So we're even. I just don't know if it's worth the trouble for me to get in there and have a look around."

"That room was barely big enough for two people," Clint said. "I doubt he'd be in there if he's got his own men and some prisoners with him. He's probably somewhere else by now."

Suddenly, Mia turned on her heels and started heading for another door. "There's a few places I want to check," she said. "While I was looking around last night, I saw some suspicious men spending a lot of time in places where there shouldn't have been much going on."

"A boat full of gamblers and you only found a few suspicious men?" Clint asked.

"Suspicious, armed, and not playing cards," she clarified.

"That is suspicious."

"Since there's two of us now, there's no reason for us to stay together every second. One of us should check out those places I found, and the other should check on room number one."

"Why room number one?" Clint asked.

"That note, DCRM1, remember? Isn't RM short for room?"

Realizing he'd somehow let that slip past him made Clint feel like an ass. Keeping his best poker face on, he nodded and said, "You can check that one out after you tell me where those places you found were. If those men are armed, I'd rather be the one to face them."

She nodded and then patted his cheek. "It's all right, Clint. I'm sure you were just in a hurry to get your arm back around Gretchen or you wouldn't have missed that."

Clint decided his poker face needed a little work.

THIRTY-ONE

Apart from the fact that he'd somehow overlooked something as obvious as RM1 meaning room number one, Clint had an even better reason for wanting to switch tasks with Mia. It was a good way for him to check out her information while allowing her to check on his. He didn't really feel too bad about telling her what he'd found on that note, since he might not have done anything with it until it was too late anyhow.

There were three spots that had caught Mia's attention. One was the furnace. Another was a storage room off the main kitchen. The third was a good-sized structure on the middle deck, close to the paddle wheel. Considering that the main kitchen was probably in use at the moment, Clint put that one and the furnace off for a while and headed for the room at the rear of the boat.

Before he headed in that direction, Clint stopped in his room to change back into his suit. That way, if anyone asked any questions, he could easily play the part of a gambler who'd lost his direction. The longer coat also made it much easier for him to hide his gun from any of the armed men who were looking to disarm the passengers.

Clint tipped his hat and put on the best smile he could

manage as he passed other gamblers and a few men who actually kept the boat running. It was a beautiful day, so the *Misty Morning* was making good time moving along the Red River. Once the paddle wheel slowed down a bit, Clint intended on checking out the furnace. For the moment, however, the noise from the churning water was just what he needed to cover his approach to the small structure at the rear of the boat.

It took a while for Clint to find the spot Mia had told him about. The directions had seemed simple enough when she told them to him, but Clint soon began to wonder if he was remembering them incorrectly somehow. After his second trip around the deck, all he had found was a few doors leading to the poker rooms and some wooden walls separating him from the paddle wheel.

On the third trip, Clint spotted a small hole on one of those paddle-wheel walls. At first, he'd thought that hole was just an imperfection in the wood, but then he realized that that side of the paddle wheel was wider than the other side. Since riverboats generally weren't built that way, Clint figured he'd found his structure.

When he examined the wall around that hole, he eventually found the recessed hinge of a door. Placing his ear against the wall, Clint could hear something else beneath the constant sound of the turning wheel.

"If you . . . your mouth . . . ," a voice on the other side of the wall said, "I'll kill . . . dump . . . overboard."

Clint's hand moved aside his jacket so he could place his hand on the grip of his Colt. He didn't need to hear every word that had been said to know that he'd found the right place. He also knew he needed to move quickly before the situation got any worse for whoever was inside.

With his one hand still on his pistol, Clint stretched out his free hand and knocked on the wall.

A few more voices came from the other side, but they were too quick and too hushed for Clint to make out what they were saying. Just to be safe, however, he stepped away from the wall so his back was to the paddle wheel.

The wall shook a little and a section of it swung inward less than an inch. Clint was standing at the wrong angle to be able to see inside, so he waited there without moving a muscle.

After a few seconds, the door's hinges squeaked again. The section of wall swung in a bit more, and a man stuck his head out to get a look around. Since most of the boat was to his right, that's where the man turned. Clint was standing to his left and wasted no time before grabbing the man by his tussled hair and pulling him out of the hidden room.

"What the hell?" the man said in surprise.

Clint kept pulling until he got a look at the man's whole body. Once he saw the gun gripped in the man's hand, Clint turned so he could direct the top of the man's head toward the railing behind him. Skull met iron with a satisfying clang. When Clint let go of the man's hair, the man staggered and fell awkwardly onto his backside.

Stepping in front of the door, Clint managed to get a quick look inside. There were several large tools hanging from the walls, one man tied to a chair and one other standing there with a rifle in his hands. Clint moved away from the doorway as soon as he saw that rifle, and just managed to clear it before a shot was fired from the room.

Although Clint could hear the distinctive crack of a gunshot, most of that sound was swallowed up by the paddle wheel, which was only a yard or two away. Clint looked around to see if anyone else was coming or if someone had heard the shot.

There wasn't a window allowing the back poker room to look at the paddle wheel, so nobody in there could have seen anything. As far as Clint could tell, the rest of the deck in the vicinity was clear, so he shifted his attention back to the more important matter of staying alive.

The first man was still shaking off the effects of being knocked headfirst into the railing. He staggered to his feet and quickly realized he'd dropped the gun he'd been holding.

The second man wasn't so quick to charge out of the room. In fact, it looked as though he wasn't even going to leave his spot. "Who the hell's out there?" he shouted from inside the room. "You come any closer and this man in here with me's gonna die!"

Clint had been standing with his back against the wall, which he now knew was the side wall of that hidden room. With his ear pressed against the wall, he was able to get a feel for where the man inside was standing. Pressing the Colt's barrel against the wall, Clint adjusted his aim and pulled the trigger. The shot was a bit louder than the rifle shot, but most of it was still washed out by the paddle wheel.

Before the man inside could do anything, Clint hurried through the door and into the little room. Just as he'd figured, his shot had punched a hole through two walls, but was too high and wide to hit anyone. It did, however, come close enough to put a fright into the rifleman.

Clint moved toward the rifleman and took a swing at him before he had a chance to think better about the idea. His fist knocked squarely into the man's jaw, sending him backward to trip over the fellow tied to a chair. As his back hit the wall, it looked as if he was going to fall down and fire a shot from his rifle, but he caught himself before doing either.

The man tied to the chair sputtered and squirmed as all of this was happening around him. Mostly, he pulled his head down and tried to curl up just to keep away from the guns and fists being thrown around so close to him.

Clint turned sideways and stretched out his left arm to grab the rifleman's shirt front and slam him once more into the wall. The man still didn't drop his rifle.

Catching a glimpse of movement from the corner of his

eye, Clint turned in that direction and was just in time to see the first man standing there. There was a red line running down the middle of that man's face and blood dripping from his nose. He scowled at Clint and brought up his pistol.

Clint's right arm snapped out in that direction and fired out of pure instinct. He then pulled his gun arm in to crack the handle of the Colt against the rifleman's forehead to finally drop that man to the floor.

Hearing steps knocking against the deck nearby, Clint hurried out of the room to find the first man still wobbling there. The man's eyes were rolled up into his head, and he was only upright because of the rail behind him. Clint could hear several people hurrying around the corner, so he pushed the standing corpse over the rail, ducked back into the room and shut the door.

THIRTY-TWO

"Please help me," the man tied to the chair groaned.

Clint was pressed against the wall and waved toward the sound of the man's voice. He turned toward the fellow in the chair just long enough to whisper, "Shut up and sit still."

After seeing what he'd just seen, the man was content for a little while longer to stay in his chair and not squirm against his ropes.

Clint turned so his face was once again pressed against the wall. That way, he was able to get a look outside through the bullet hole he'd created less than a minute ago. The hole wasn't too big, but it was enough to allow him to see three men in dark clothes rush around the corner. Clint could also feel those men's footsteps as they walked closer and closer to the wall.

"Are you sure you heard something over here?" one of the men asked.

Although the second man was standing closer to the wall, he was standing too close for Clint to get a look at him. Instead, Clint could hear the man shuffling back and forth less than a foot away from him.

"I heard something," the second man said. "Didn't you?"

"What?"

Raising his voice to be heard over the paddle wheel and churning water, the man asked, "Didn't you hear anything?"

"I thought I heard something, but I don't know what the hell it was. For all I know it was some kid hunting squirrels on the shore somewhere."

Clint could feel the second man moving around. It wasn't anything concrete, but more of the sort of feeling someone got when he knew he was being watched. Closing his eyes, Clint eased his boot against the door to hold it shut if someone tried to push it open.

After a tense couple of seconds, the man stepped directly in front of the hole Clint was looking through.

"I can't even hear myself think so close to this goddamn wheel," he grunted.

There were more steps knocking against the deck nearby, but Clint couldn't hear much more than that.

Apparently, the first man heard something else, because he turned and shouted, "It's nothing. Just like I said it was."

"Let's go play some cards before someone steals the money I had on the table," the man closest to the wall grunted.

After that, all those sets of footsteps moved away from the room until they were swallowed up by the constant sound of the paddle wheel.

Clint turned away from the wall so he could get a look at the man tied to the chair. That man looked like he was in his early twenties, but still outweighed Clint by at least thirty pounds. Sweat rolled down his face and glistened in the dim light cast by a single, sputtering lantern that was burning just enough to remain lit.

"Are you going to kill me?" the man asked.

"I was thinking about getting you out of those ropes," Clint replied. "How's that sound?"

The man nodded with his mouth agape, as if he was waiting for the offer to be retracted at any moment.

Since he didn't have a knife on him, Clint set about loosening the ropes the old-fashioned way. As his fingers dug into the knots, he spoke to the man in the chair in the calmest voice he could manage.

"What's your name?" Clint asked.

"Marty."

"You're a gambler, Marty?"

"Yes, sir."

"No need for the formalities. My name's Clint. Even though I'm not going to hurt you, I'd appreciate it if you kept your voice down just in case any more of these assholes come back around to check on their friends."

That seemed to put Marty's mind at ease. Feeling his hands start to come free also gave him a boost of confidence as he straightened up and spoke in a quicker rush of words. "Who the hell are these guys? Why'd they come after me? I don't even know who they are!"

"Remember the deal, Marty. Keep quiet."

"Oh, yeah."

"Sit still and I'll have you out in a bit." As he pulled on the knot that Marty had just tightened thanks to his sudden movements, Clint asked, "What happened to land you in here?"

"I was doing well at a table and one of the men asked me to have a cigar with him outside. The next thing I know, some other big fellows jumped me and hit me on the head. When I woke up, I was here."

"That's all you remember?"

"Apart from being stuffed in here while they threatened me, that's all there was."

"Did they hurt you at all?" Clint asked.

"They knocked me around some, but it wasn't as bad as the knock to the head. That still hurts like hell."

"Good," Clint said as he stood up. "Then you can stand

up and help me lift this fellow up so he can take your place."

Marty stood up slowly. When the ropes dropped away from him, he looked as if he might give Clint a grateful bear hug.

"He might be coming around," Clint said as a way to stop the hug before it got started.

Marty turned his enthusiasm toward the man on the floor and did most of the work in lifting him up. When he dropped him onto the chair, Marty was looking right into the man's face as he started to groan and open his eyes.

Before Clint could lift a finger, Marty slammed his fist into the man's face and dropped him right back into unconsciousness.

"How do you like that?" Marty said to the man who was already slumping into the chair.

Clint had the ropes in hand and started looping them around the new prisoner.

THIRTY-THREE

Mia hurried to the hallway leading to room number one. There were plenty of hallways throughout the riverboat, but most of them were short and skinny. Only one on each deck ran the entire length of the boat, and this wasn't one of them. In fact, this hallway barely ran for more than a few paces and only led to one door.

That door, however, had a small number one painted on it. It also had two large men with guns at their hips nearly blocking her view.

After a quick look down that hall, Mia put on a large smile and, with her hands held behind her back, walked toward the door and its guards.

"Well, well," she said sweetly. "What have we here?"

Although both of the men took a moment to look her over, only one of them spoke.

"Are you looking for someone?" he asked.

"Sure. I'm looking for two big, strong men to give me something to do since everyone else is obsessed with playing cards all day long. You think you can help me with that?"

They both chuckled, but the spokesman shook his head. "Maybe later. You should probably move along."

"What about the man in that room? Maybe he'd like to play with me?"

"Mr. Crane is getting ready for a private game, and it's not the sort you're after."

Having made her way all they way up to the guards, Mia reached out to place one hand flat against each of their chests. She rubbed them up and down, while shifting her eyes back and forth between them. "How do you know what I'm after?" she purred.

"I think I can hazard a guess."

Her eyes narrowed a bit, and she pursed her lips as if she couldn't decide whether she wanted to say something or give him a kiss. Finally, she whispered, "You could always let me in so I could ask him myself."

The guard seemed to take a moment to consider the offer. Either that, or he was just enjoying having Mia so close to him. Reluctantly, he told her, "I don't think so, ma'am. You should probably leave."

The second guard jumped in by offering, "You could always come back a little later. I'll bet one of us would be more'n happy to oblige you with a game or two."

"Really?" Mia whispered as she sauntered in between the two guards. She kept her hands on both of them until she was within an inch of the door. Suddenly, she turned around and then replaced her hands upon both men's chests. "Why wait until later?"

Even the guard who'd been speaking in a stern, controlled voice the entire time looked as if he might choke when he heard that. He glanced between her and his partner without being able to get a word out of his mouth.

The second guard, on the other hand, wasn't having the same sort of trouble. "What do you have in mind, sweetie?" he asked.

Mia never took her eyes off the men's faces. When she wasn't looking one in the eyes, she was staring down the other. The intensity in those glares was almost enough on its own to put both men under her command.

"We can't just . . . ," the first guard sputtered.

"I can take care of both of you right here," Mia said. "Since one of you is a little nervous, I can start with the one who's more willing."

"That'd be me," the second guard said as he took a step closer to her.

The first guard gritted his teeth and fixed his eyes upon his partner as if he was going to knock the other man's head clean off his shoulders. Before he could say or do a thing, Mia was already in motion.

Both of her hands dropped down to the guards' gun belts. She plucked each man's gun from its holster with so much ease that she was able to raise them, aim one at each man's face and thumb the hammers back.

Taking a few quick steps away from the door, Mia put herself out of the guards' reach and was able to keep an eye on both of them at the same time.

"What the fuck is this?" the second guard grunted.

Keeping her feet planted and her guns pointed at both men's heads, she replied, "The last day of your lives if you don't play your cards right."

The first guard barely even moved his lips as he snarled, "You're dead."

"Is that what you said to the people in those banks you robbed? Or what about the men who came after those horses you stole?" she asked the second guard. "Did you have anything to say to them? I know who both of you are: Pete Northern and Don McNabb."

Just seeing the surprised look on those two men's faces was more than enough to tell Mia she was on the right track. Of course, recognizing them from wanted posters displayed by the Texas Rangers didn't hurt.

"I also know you're working for Jack Solomon," she

said. That statement was a slight gamble, but it quickly paid off.

"So you know," McNabb, the first guard, said. "So what?"

"So when were you going to move on Daryl Crane?" Mia asked.

The guards looked back and forth at each other, with McNabb fiercely glaring to keep Pete silent.

"It's all right," Mia said. "You don't have to say anything anymore. You look like guilty bastards and that's just what you are. Practically every big player on this boat knew Crane was coming, so that was no secret."

"So what the hell do you want from us?" McNabb asked.

"Tell me everything that Solomon has planned and I might consider letting you go."

"No, you won't."

"How can you be so sure?" Mia asked.

McNabb smirked and replied, "Because you're the law, and no law in their right mind would let us go."

"Maybe I'm not the law."

"If you weren't, you woulda shot by now."

When Mia smirked, it wiped the grin right off of McNabb's face. "Then maybe I'm not in my right mind."

"What you gonna do now?" Pete asked. "Sooner or later someone will come along and see you with them guns in your hands."

"Guess I'd better put them to use, then," Mia said. "Unless you want to strike a deal and tell me what I want to know."

After saying that, Mia didn't make a move.

McNabb, on the other hand, dropped down for the backup holster strapped to his boot, and Pete followed suit by reaching for his jacket pocket.

Mia pulled both of her triggers, sending a bullet into Pete first and then dropping McNabb.

As the bodies were falling, the door was pulled open and a distinguished-looking gentleman looked out from his room.

"Mr. Crane?" Mia said as she approached him with a smoking gun in each hand. "We need to talk."

THIRTY-FOUR

When Clint and Mia met up again, each of them was surprised to find that the other wasn't alone. Clint walked into Mia's room with Marty in tow. Since the room wasn't much bigger than his, and there were now four people in it, closing the door suddenly became a challenge.

Mia got up so Marty could sit next to Crane, while Clint took a spot close to the door. Introductions were quickly made, and then Clint and Mia both swapped stories as to what they'd been doing since they split up. When they were done, Mia asked, "Can you think of a better place to hide these two?"

"Sure," Clint replied. "Anywhere off of this boat."

"But there's not a stop scheduled until we're on our way back up the river. And Solomon will have made his move by then."

"You still don't even know what, exactly, that move is going to be," Clint pointed out.

Mia started to speak. She wanted to speak. She even made a second attempt to speak, but she finally wound up shaking her head. "I know what he wants to do, but you're right. I still don't know exactly how he's going to do it."

"I'll bet I know someone who does," Clint said.

"Really?"

Clint nodded and looked over to the two men sitting on the cot. "Tell us what happened, who did this to you and what they said."

Both Crane and Marty looked surprised.

"I already told you what happened," Marty said. "That's all I can remember."

"What about you?" Clint asked. "What do you remember, Mr. Crane?"

Crane looked to be a bit older than his years, but that was mainly due to the way he carried himself. A narrow goatee made his face seem longer and sharper than it truly was, and spectacles perched on his nose gave him a book-ish quality that made him seem better suited for a library than a poker game.

Still, when Crane opened his mouth to speak, he delivered the goods. "Jack Solomon is the man who tried to kill me," he said.

Clint and Mia both turned to him and fixed all of their attention on what he was saying.

"You were just being held prisoner," Mia pointed out. "Are you certain you were going to be killed?"

"Oh, yes," Crane replied.

"And you're certain Jack Solomon is the man behind it?"

"Most definitely. I recognized him."

"You saw him?" Mia asked as some of the excitement came back into her voice.

Crane nodded. "He approached me almost as soon as I came on board. He said he knew all about my lumber business and would burn every last one of my mills to the ground if I didn't hand over every bit of money I brought with me to this tournament."

"How did he know how much money you had?" Clint asked.

"I don't know," Crane said, "but it's a substantial amount. He said I was to lose it all to him and a few other men he pointed out, and I would never hear from him again."

"So why do you think he was going to kill you?" Clint asked.

"I could see it in his eyes. He was lying to me when he said he'd let me go. He was lying when he said he just wanted the money I brought to gamble with. He wasn't lying, however, when he said I wouldn't hear from him again. I assume that was a sick joke since I wouldn't hear from anyone after I was killed."

"That's a lot to figure out from that one conversation," Clint said.

"Do you play poker, sir?"

"Yes."

"Then you know it's in a player's best interests to figure out as much as he can in as little time as possible. I've played cards with Solomon before. That's how I recognized him now. He's a proficient liar, but he was barely even trying this time around. I guessed that was because he had no intention of letting me out of this room. At least, not alive."

Clint studied the scholarly man for a few seconds. What threw him off the most was how calm Crane appeared to be. He sat with his back straight and his hands folded on his lap as if he was simply waiting for another appointment. Not even Crane's glasses moved from their spot perched on the bridge of his nose.

"Can you tell me what Solomon looks like?" Mia asked.

Crane looked over to her, blinked and said, "I assure you, it was him."

"I believe you. It's just that . . ." She trailed off and nervously glanced over to Clint. Letting out a reluctant sigh, she said, "I just need to be able to spot him."

"You don't know his face?" Clint asked.

"I don't think any of the Rangers know his face."

"I could draw him out in a card game," Crane said. "But

you'd have to be able to keep a close watch to make sure I don't wind up right back where I was."

Clint shook his head. "Too risky."

"They might not kill me if they know I've got protection. Solomon bought off the fellows that were supposed to guard me."

"I know they'll kill me," Marty said. "They were going to try to get a ransom from my family, but they were gonna kill me. There's no way those bastards would have just taken the money and let me go, pretty as you please."

Clint grinned and flinched when he heard that. "Oh yeah," he said. "There might be someone else who can help us."

"Who?"

"One of the men who was guarding Marty is still alive."

Mia rubbed her eyes and moaned. "If Solomon hasn't already found him by now."

"I doubt anyone's found him yet."

THIRTY-FIVE

The poker room at the front of the boat wasn't as noisy as the one in the back, but it was just as small. With windows spread across three of the four walls, all six of the room's tables were flooded with light as well as a splendid view of the river. Only two games were being held in that room, but the men at the tables didn't seem too concerned with their cards or the spectacular view.

"How the hell could they both be gone?" Solomon asked.

The men at his table were all on Solomon's payroll, and they laid their cards down so they could be ready for any whim their employer might have.

Dench sat at the second table. He shook his head and tossed in a few more pennies to cover his bet.

A man stood next to Solomon, wearing the uniform of the boat's crew. There was no insignia on his shoulders or chest, but instead the coal stains and calluses on his hands marked him as someone who worked below the decks. He wiped his hands on a cloth and shrugged his shoulders. "I'm just telling you what I found when I went to check on the others," he said. "The tool shed at the back of the boat was empty. Some people said they heard a shot or two, but wouldn't swear by it. Crane's cabin was a mess. At least, the outside of it was."

"What do you mean by that?"

The uniformed man shifted on his feet and looked around to the others in the room as if he was waiting for someone to save him from drowning. "The two men that were watching Crane are . . . They're dead."

Solomon ground his teeth together as he looked down at the cards he'd been playing. There were no chips or money of any kind on his table. Instead, he'd been playing gin with his men. After sifting through his cards one more time, he set them down again and pushed his chair a little ways from the table. "What do I pay you for?" he asked.

The uniformed man raised his hands and replied, "The man being held down below is still right where he should be. I was just making the rounds to check on the other two."

"And I suppose there wasn't anything you could do?"

"No! It was already done, Mr. Solomon!"

"And there was no way for you to know this was happening? Don't any of the other crew members spread news like that around?"

"There isn't much of a crew," the uniformed man said. "Half of them are already working for you and the other half are doing their jobs to keep the boat moving. Considering how many of those are in this room right now, it's a wonder we haven't run aground."

A few of the men at the tables shifted nervously in their seats. They were wearing uniforms as well, but their clothes didn't show half the wear of those worn by the man speaking to Solomon.

After glancing at those men for himself, Solomon nodded and said, "Fine. What did you find when you went to check on the other two?"

"Like I said, there were two dead men inside room number one. Crane was gone. The tool shed at the back of the boat was empty. There was a bullet hole in the wall, but no blood that I could see."

"That's it?"

"That's it."

Solomon's frustration showed on his face. His hands were clenched into fists, but he relaxed them and said, "We're not completely unprepared for this. We'll just have to round up replacements for the people we lost. You men," he said while snapping toward the other table. "Go get another two from the list and bring them to join the other one."

"Is that a good idea?" the man in the dirty uniform asked. "Someone might still check in on us down there."

"Then we won't let them. Besides, we won't need much time. I'll arrange to start up a big game tonight, and while I'm playing, we can smuggle our three guests off the boat. It was going to happen anyway, so it's just a matter of making it sooner rather than later."

Hearing that, a few of the men seated at the tables got up and left the room. Dench was one of those who stood, but he stayed behind for a few seconds longer.

"I want to know who's behind this kink in the plan," Solomon said. "Whoever answers that question will get double their cut. Whoever allows another kink to develop will not live to see the next sunrise."

That caused the rest of the men to get up and hurry out of the room. Only Solomon, Dench and the man in the dirty uniform remained.

"Go back and keep a close watch on your prisoner. Fortify your position and prepare for the others."

"What if whoever killed those men comes down there?"

"Then you kill him," Solomon said. "Take Dench with you. He knows what to do if things go wrong."

Dench grinned and held open the door for the uniformed man, who walked out of the room like he was being led to the gallows.

THIRTY-SIX

Clint and Mia walked arm in arm along the deck. They moved at a brisk pace, but not brisk enough to catch the attention of any of the others who were out for a walk as well. With the poker games in full swing, the *Misty Morning* seemed close to deserted. Its decks were all but empty, but every window was glowing with light.

Inside the riverboat, it was a completely different story. Music was being played, and voices were rolling through the air. Fists slammed against tables, and stacks of chips were being pushed back and forth. Money was no longer allowed in the pots, simply because there was too much of it being thrown around.

"How come there's no more cash on the tables?" Mia asked as they walked past a window looking in on a game.

Clint tipped his hat to the men who looked outside. "It's supposed to keep folks from getting bad ideas about grabbing some of that money and running off with it."

"They could grab the chips."

"Sure, but then they'd still have to cash them in. Anyone who hadn't missed their chips and come after them by then deserves to lose them. At least, that's the general idea."

Clint came to a stop within sight of the paddle wheel.

They were on the same deck as the one where he'd found Marty, and they now stopped as if to take in some of the scenery.

"Is that it?" Mia asked.

"Yep. Is there anyone around?"

Mia looked around and even backtracked a few steps to get a look around the corner. When she came back to Clint's side, she shook her head. "Sounds like they're serving supper."

"Between that and the games kicking in, I'd say we've got this deck to ourselves for a little while."

"I thought you said there was a shed around here."

Clint walked toward the wall next to the paddle wheel. Now that he knew what was there, it was a wonder that he'd ever missed it before. "This is it," he told her as he reached out to touch the bullet hole in the wall. He led Mia around to the door and pushed it open. After all that had happened earlier, the door was wedged shut rather than locked.

Mia stepped forward and looked into the narrow little space. Her eyes wandered along the walls and the long rods that hung there. Piled in one corner was a set of nets, hooks and pikes that tapered down to the same rounded attachment.

Turning back to Clint, she asked, "I thought you said there was someone tied up in here. Where is he?"

Clint was leaning against the rail with his arms folded. "This is the first place I knew someone would be coming to look," he said. "Why would I leave him right there?"

"Where else can you take him? What the hell is this even here for anyway?"

"Near as I can figure," Clint said as he walked into the shack, "these poles are meant to clean off the paddle wheel or clear off anything that got snagged on it." He took one of the poles off the wall, picked up a hook from the corner and screwed it onto the end of the pole. "I was going to tie him to his chair, but then I thought the same thing you did. Check outside again for me."

Growing more frustrated by the second, Mia stepped out and took another quick look around. When she came back, she said, "Nobody's around."

Clint stepped out with the pole in hand and went to the rail. "Then I figured I might as well use the tools I've got."

When she saw where Clint was looking, Mia glanced there and then shook her head. "You didn't."

Clint nodded and leaned over the rail while reaching down even farther with the hook. Mia leaned over as well and immediately saw the man about three feet down, hanging from a steel post that looked like it was intended to hold a flag.

The man dangled by his wrists, which were tied by a thick length of rope. He'd been hanging just below the sight of anyone on that deck and just above the deck below. He wasn't moving a muscle, since he'd already managed to slip to the very end of the post. He didn't even kick or struggle when Clint reached down with the hook, since doing so could very well have knocked his legs against the churning paddle wheel.

After a try or two, Clint got the hook between the man's wrists and started to pull him up. Not only did the man allow himself to be hooked, but he grabbed onto the hook with his fingers and fought to swing his legs toward the rail as soon as it was close enough. As he got closer, his voice could be heard shouting from behind the gag that Clint had wrapped around his mouth. That sound, like most of the others that close to the wheel, couldn't be heard over the splash of water.

"Give him a hand," Clint said calmly.

Mia reached out and grabbed the man's jacket so she could work to haul him up. He landed with a wet thump, and before he could catch his breath, he was pulled up to his feet by Clint.

"You ready to talk?" Clint asked, "or do you want to enjoy the view from the back of the boat some more?"

"No, no!" the man shouted. "Don't put me back there again!"

"Then you're gonna have to tell me—" Clint stopped talking as he felt Mia tap him frantically on the shoulder. When he looked over to her, he saw her point toward the deck, where some people were headed their way.

Before the trembling man could get a look at who was coming, Clint wrapped his arm around him and turned so they were both at the rail, facing the river. As the people slowly walked by behind them, Clint asked, "You remember your friend? He went over this same rail, but he's still facedown at the bottom of the river."

"I . . . I'll tell you whatever you want. I just want to get off this boat. Please. I'll even tell you where to find one of the women Solomon had his eye on."

The man was broken.

Clint didn't like seeing anyone like that, but at least both of them were still alive. "All right," he said. "Let's get you somewhere else you can wait out the rest of this ride."

"Thank you," the man stammered. "Thank you."

THIRTY-SEVEN

Clint couldn't decide if it was all that river air, all that river water or all that hanging by his fingers that had gotten the gunman to change his tune. All that mattered was that he did change his tune in a big way. Once Clint got him tied to a nice chair inside a dry cabin, the man opened up like he was Clint's best friend.

In fact, he told Clint twice as much as he'd hoped to hear. When the man was finished, he let Clint tie the gag around his mouth just so he could rest his eyes without the threat of falling into a paddle wheel. In a strange sort of way, Clint actually felt sorry for him.

Clint most certainly did not feel sorry for the big fellow who was standing outside the small poker room at the front of the *Misty Morning*. He walked straight up to the bulky guard and said, "Let me inside."

"You ain't invited."

"How do I get invited?" Clint asked. "Hold a rich man hostage and ransom him back to his family?"

The man at the door squinted once as if he didn't know quite what to do. He didn't pause much more than that before reaching for the gun at his side. Clint's hand flashed forward to clamp down and pin the man's hand on top of

147

his gun. Clint's free hand balled into a fist, which was then delivered straight into the doorman's face.

The doorman was a big man, so his head knocked into the door with a lot of noise, and enough force to push the door open. He was going to swing at Clint, but he was already staggering backward into the poker room. Clint followed him in and took a quick look at what he was dealing with inside.

Mia had figured this would be where a lot of Solomon's men could be found, and the gunman who'd suddenly decided to spill his guts to Clint after hanging off the back of the boat concurred. Clint wasn't quite ready to risk his life on the word of that gunman, but he figured this would be a good chance to see how much truth was in his words. It turned out that the gunman's description had been pretty close.

But that description didn't matter. Clint knew he couldn't walk straight up to Solomon without knowing what he looked like, and he wouldn't be able to ask around very long with all of Solomon's men waiting to shoot him.

Clint had to thin the herd and this was just the place to do it.

For the first second or two that Clint was in the room, the other four men already in there were stunned. Two were at a table playing cards, and another two were leaning against a small bar situated in front of a few shelves of bottles. When Clint saw Elsa tied up in the corner, he knew he had the right place.

And in the next blink of an eye, everything went to hell.

The two men at the bar were already on their feet, so it was easier for them to turn toward Clint while drawing their guns. They were both equally fast at clearing leather, but one of them raised his gun just a little ahead of the other. Clint spotted this difference immediately and unleashed a storm of lead at that man first.

Clint's first round hit its target in the chest. His second

was only an inch or two to the left. Rather than try to pause and take better aim, Clint fired a third shot toward the bar and began sidestepping before return fire could head his way.

That return fire came soon enough. The first round hissed through the air to Clint's left, and the following rounds would have struck home if they hadn't been intercepted along the way. Just as Clint had planned, it was the doorman's body that did the intercepting. Clint had stepped behind that man just as he'd drawn his pistol, and bullets from the man at the bar drilled into the doorman's torso.

By this time, both men at the table had stood up and drawn their weapons. One of them started firing first, but his shots were wild and thumped into the wall a few feet from where Clint was standing.

The second man took his time and sighted along his barrel until he had a clear shot. His finger tightened around his trigger when he saw Clint step away from the doorman's body. Unfortunately for. him, that gave Clint more than enough time to aim and fire a round right back at him. The second man at the table flew backward off his feet and landed in a dead heap upon the floor.

Two men remained.

Despite the chaos and thunder that filled the room, those last two gunmen kept their wits about them and even circled around to get Clint into a cross fire.

Clint knew he only had two bullets remaining and his cover was finally about to drop over. The doorman wobbled on his feet, having been kept upright this long thanks to Clint's grip upon the back of his jacket. Clint let go of the doorman, dropped to one knee, scooped up the pistol the doorman had dropped and fired a round from each gun in his hands.

Both pistols barked at the same time. The bullet from Clint's Colt hit the second man at the card table right between the eyes. The bullet from the doorman's gun wasn't as accurate, but it took down its target all the same. One man slumped against the bar and the other fell face-first onto the card table.

After that, the room was completely silent.

Clint got to his feet and looked around to make sure he hadn't missed anything. All the gunmen were down, and Elsa was huddled in the corner. Clint walked over to her, then reloaded and holstered the Colt before kneeling to untie her.

"Are you all right?" he asked after taking the gag from her mouth.

The moment her hands were free, Elsa wrapped her arms around Clint and gave him a big kiss. "That," she said between more kisses, "was . . . great!"

Clint accepted the kisses, but pulled her to her feet. "We'd better get out of here," he said.

"Oh, yes. I don't want to see another card table for a long time."

As they walked out, Clint saw several gamblers and crew members rushing down the hall toward them. A gambler dressed in a pearl gray suit led the way. "What the hell happened?" he asked. "Were those gunshots?"

"Someone got caught palming an ace," Clint said. He then walked through the small group, taking Elsa with him.

It didn't take long before whispers of "just desserts" started drifting down the narrow hall.

THIRTY-EIGHT

Clint could feel Elsa trembling the entire time they were
walking away from that poker room. He held her hand and
pulled her along, saying, "Just a little farther. Try to look
normal."

He figured she was frightened after what had happened,
or nervous from being in the middle of all that shooting.
Since he could feel her grip on his hand tightening by the
second, he hurried up and tried to find somewhere private
so he could talk to her without anyone else listening in.

"Where are you taking me?" she asked.

"My cabin's not far. I thought we could—"

"No," she said as she changed direction and pulled Clint
toward another set of stairs, leading upward. "My cabin's
closer. It's right up here."

Clint followed her to a door at the top of the stairs and to
a room with several portholes overlooking the front of the
riverboat. "Are you hurt?" he asked once they were inside
the room.

Elsa shut the door and rushed toward Clint with a fire in
her eyes. She clasped his face in her hands and pressed her
lips against his with a burning intensity that made Clint's

151

heart race almost as it had done when the lead was flying around him.

"I'm not hurt," she said quickly as she pulled back just enough to start pulling off Clint's jacket. "I'm doing just fine, and in a second, I'll be doing even better." She pulled his shirt open, ran her hands over his chest and added, "So will you."

"There's not enough time for—"

"There's time," she interrupted. "There's always time. Solomon won't be starting his game for another hour. I heard those assholes talking after they tied me up. If I don't get you right now, I swear I'll burn up."

Clint felt like he was riding the crest of a tidal wave. In fact, he felt like he was still riding through the same storm that had started along with all the shooting. Only now, he'd just been swept even higher into the air.

Giving in to the rush that flowed through him, Clint unbuckled his belt and pushed Elsa against a wall. "Damn, your sister was right," he said. "You are the wild one."

"You have no idea."

Elsa hiked up her skirt and propped one foot on a nearby chair. There was a slip beneath her skirt, and when she pulled that aside, she showed Clint that she wasn't wearing anything else. Her strawberry blond hair fell over her face as she locked eyes with Clint, silently commanding him to do her bidding.

Clint was more than happy to oblige, since his mind was running along the same set of tracks. He stepped between her open legs, reached around to take hold of her firm buttocks and then guided his rigid cock into her.

When he pushed his hips forward, Clint slid easily between the wet lips of her pussy. Elsa pulled in a deep breath, until he was all the way inside of her. Her back was arched, and her nails clawed at Clint so hard that he thought they might have drawn blood. That didn't matter, since the pleasure he felt was more than enough to distract him from the pain.

Now that he was inside of her, Clint had both hands free to roam over her body as he pumped in and out of her. One hand settled upon her buttocks, so he could feel her muscles tense every time he drove into her. The other hand moved up and down her thigh before finding its way back to her firm breasts.

Elsa arched her back and wriggled her hips slightly to make sure Clint hit all the right spots. When she found the perfect angle, she clenched her eyes shut and trembled as a little orgasm rippled through her. When it passed, she opened her eyes and began grinding against Clint even harder as she moaned all the way from the back of her throat.

Clint reached under her skirts with both hands so he could grab hold of her tight, bare buttocks. Every time he pumped forward, he pulled her closer. Elsa let out a passionate groan every time she felt him drive into her. She then spread her legs even more, as if to urge him to go even deeper.

Clint pumped until he felt her tightening around him. When he climaxed, he thrust a few more times, until he felt Elsa trembling again. They shuddered against each other until they caught their breath. Even after that, it took a while before Clint's head stopped spinning.

THIRTY-NINE

Clint rushed back to his room with Elsa following him. He pushed open the door to find the cabin crowded, but still short by one person. "Where's Mia?" he asked.

Crane sat perched upon the only chair that didn't have someone tied to it. "She hasn't been back yet," he replied. "Who's this?"

"What do you mean she hasn't been back? Where did she go?"

"She mentioned something about checking one last place for anyone else who might be in trouble. She told me to tell you she'd return shortly."

"How long ago was that?"

Thinking it over for a second, Crane replied, "Twenty minutes."

Clint looked around to some of the others in the room. Marty shrugged and said, "Twenty minutes sounds about right. She was loaded for bear, so I wouldn't worry about her too much."

"Keep an eye on things while I'm gone," Clint said.

Marty nodded. "Will do."

"I was talking to her," Clint said as he ushered Elsa into the cabin.

As Clint hurried through the decks and hallways of the *Misty Morning*, he felt as if he hadn't stopped running through that boat since he'd stepped foot on it. Since he'd crawled, run or fought on nearly every inch of the river-boat, he felt as if the vessel had shrunken in size. Now that he knew the boat backward and forward, it seemed more like a box floating along a strip of water than the three-level monster it was.

And yet, despite his familiarity with the *Misty Morning*, it seemed to take him forever to run all the way down to the lower deck and start looking for the room containing the furnace. He knew that's where Mia had to be headed. It was the one place on her list of suspicious places that nei-ther of them had covered yet.

Clint thought he'd had an understanding with her that they would go there together. In fact, he even felt uncom-fortable going there now. The whole reason for waiting was to let the heat cool off after all these confrontations so the remaining gunmen could settle into one spot where they could be easily found.

Apparently, Mia was tired of waiting. Clint only hoped that lack of patience was her only problem at the moment. Since he hadn't caught sight of Dench since their run-in at the laundry, Clint knew that jumping the gun could very well prove to be a big problem for Mia.

By the time he reached the lower deck and was follow-ing the sound of clanging metal and the smell of burning coal to its source, Clint had gone from being worried about Mia to being mad at her.

She should have known better than to take off on her own when it was so dangerous.

She should know how to stick to a plan.

She should know how to work with someone else if she was truly accustomed to working alongside the Texas Rangers.

The more he thought about how reckless she was, the

more Clint's blood boiled at the prospect of pulling her fat from the fire.

He passed the laundry in a rush. Clint's eyes were fixed upon a door at the end of the hall that was labeled as the furnace room. Compared to the halls on the upper decks, these were even more cramped and shadowy. Some light from outside drifted in, but it wasn't enough to make the hall half as welcoming as the ones that led to passenger cabins. Even the dark spots between the poker rooms seemed inviting compared to this.

When Clint saw the flicker of motion in the corner of his eye, he was barely able to turn toward it before he was pulled off balance. His hand was already on the grip of his Colt by the time he got a look at who'd reached out to yank him from the hall.

"What the hell are you doing?" Mia snapped.

Clint found himself in a dirty closet that was just big enough to hold him, Mia, a bunch of brooms and some buckets. "I was just going to ask you the same thing," he replied. "What possessed you to head down here on your own?"

"I was just taking a look to make sure there was still a reason to come back here. After all the dust we've kicked up, I wouldn't have been surprised if Solomon rearranged all his plans. Now, what in God's name were you doing stomping toward the furnace like you had a death wish?"

Clint was taken aback by the question, mainly because it mirrored the same thoughts and emotions running through his own mind. "I got back to the room and you weren't there. They told me you went to go check on something and I figured you came here."

"Did you also figure I'd go rushing into that room by myself when I knew Dench and Lord only knows how many others would be in there?" she asked.

Pausing for a moment, Clint tried to think of a way to phrase his answer that wouldn't seem ignorant. The best he could come up with on such short notice was "Yeah. I guess I did. But I was only angry because that would have been so out of character."

Mia smiled and patted his cheek. Her voice softened a bit as she said, "That's sweet."

"Enough of that," Clint said as he swatted her hand away. "What did you find out?"

Still looking at him with a teasing grin, she said, "Maybe you're a little too worked up to be here right now."

"That's enough," Clint grumbled. "I jumped the gun. Let's move on. Surely there's a reason you were hiding in this closet."

Mia nodded. "They're still in there, all right. I caught sight of a few of them coming and going in the last couple of minutes. Something must have ruffled their feathers."

"That would have been me," Clint said. "I went up to the front poker room and found a few armed men guarding it just like our friend from the flagpole told us there would be."

"Did they give you any trouble?"

"I'm surprised you didn't hear the fireworks."

The humor that had been on her face quickly went away. This time, when Mia touched him, she did so tenderly and asked, "Are you all right?"

"I took them by surprise. Let's just say that Solomon's chances of getting off this boat are seriously dwindling. How many do you think are in there?"

Shifting her eyes back to the hall and the nearby door leading into the furnace room, she said, "At least three."

"That's not so bad. There was more than that upstairs."

"One of them's Dench."

"Are you sure about that?" Clint asked.

Mia nodded. "I saw him go in there myself and he hasn't come out."

Clint took a look for himself and saw nothing but a deserted hallway. "They've got to be holed up in there and ready for a fight. I don't know everything about riverboats, but I'm pretty sure there's a way for the men down here to signal to the man at the wheel. Solomon's most likely got someone up there to catch the signal and send reinforcements if they're needed."

"And what about those men you found upstairs? Could they have been reinforcements?"

"Possibly," Clint said. "But they were guarding a prisoner. I do have an idea, though. Are there any men out there who know who you are that aren't tied up in my room?"

"Not many. Why?"

FORTY

Mia ran up to the uppermost deck, which was mostly one room, perched toward the front of the riverboat. She knocked furiously on the door and then pushed it open. As she bolted into the steering room of the boat, she saw nothing but a few men in uniform. One of them stood behind the wheel and the other two were at the front window.

"Mr. Solomon said to signal the men that are down by the furnace," she said in a rush.

For a moment, she thought that nobody in that room had a clue what she was talking about. Then, one of the men at the window asked, "And who are you?"

"I'm the one delivering the message," she replied. "And I'll be the one to tell Mr. Solomon that you didn't carry it out right away."

The man stared at her for a moment and then reached out to one of the several cords that ran down through the floor. He gave the cord three sharp, upward pulls and then looked at her again. "Anything else?"

"No," Mia said as she stepped out of the room. "That'll do."

• • •

Clint stayed hidden and watched to see if anyone would come out to chase after Mia. Even though nobody came, Clint wasn't feeling any better. As he studied the door leading into the furnace room, he began to realize why Dench had chosen that spot as a place to hole up with a few prisoners.

The door was thicker than the rest and may have been reinforced with strips of iron. If nobody wanted Clint to get inside, there was no way in hell he'd be able to force his way in. As that unsettling thought rolled around in his head, Clint heard the muffled sound of a bell clanging three times.

After the bell sounded, there were some noises from inside the furnace room, followed by the rattle of the door being unlocked. Clint hunkered down in the darkness of the closet and watched as the door swung open to let two men walk into the hall.

Clint watched those men and waited for them to draw their guns and walk straight toward him. He waited for them to shout out a threat or maybe even fire at someone he couldn't see, but none of that happened. Instead, the men walked right past Clint without so much as looking in his direction. After the men had walked a few more steps down the hall, Clint jumped from his hiding spot and drew his Colt.

"You two might want to drop your guns right about now," Clint said. "And you should do it nice and slow."

Both men turned around quickly because they were surprised by the sudden noises coming from behind them. They froze after catching a glimpse of Clint. Their hands stayed over their guns, but they didn't make a move for them. At least, they didn't move for them yet.

"You heard me," Clint said as he felt every second tick by. "Drop those guns and do it now."

The men looked at Clint, then they looked at each other. From there, they did something that Clint truly wasn't expecting. As if they'd coordinated their actions without a word passing between them, both men charged toward Clint without caring about the gun in his hand.

Since he didn't have time to wonder why they thought they could get away with such a move, Clint reacted to it instead. He turned his body to the side and took a quick step forward so he could slip between the charging attackers.

Before Clint could make another move of his own, he saw one of the men pivot and lash out with the back of his fist as his entire torso swung around. Clint did his best to dodge the blow, but still caught some of that man's fist on his chin. The impact rattled Clint's entire head and made him unsteady on his legs for a moment. That was more than enough time for the second man to turn and send a punch into Clint's ribs.

Even though he could have taken a shot at either of the men, Clint kept his finger off his trigger, in hopes of finishing the fight before anyone else inside the furnace room could shut and lock the door. As if playing out his worst fears, someone stood in that doorway and took quick stock of what was happening outside.

Clint recognized Dench's face almost immediately. In the second that they met each other's gaze, Clint couldn't decide if Dench was going to come out or dig into his hole. As soon as Dench moved back rather than forward, Clint knew the other man had chosen the latter of those two choices.

A fist slammed into Clint's side, but his blood was pumping too hard for him to feel much pain. The gunman who'd punched him in the face was now reaching for his pistol, so Clint set his sights on him first.

Clint raised the modified Colt, but didn't take a shot. Instead, he slammed the length of the barrel into the gunman's stomach, which doubled him over. As Clint straightened himself up, he lifted his knee into the gunman's chin. That blow landed with enough force to knock the gunman back hard enough to crack his head against the wall.

That left the man who'd punched Clint in the ribs. As Clint drove his elbow into that man's chest, he saw Dench retreat another step back while closing the heavy door. Clint knew damn well that he wouldn't be able to get into that room if the door was locked. He also knew that whatever hostages were in there would be dead in a matter of seconds after the lock fell into place.

Keeping his sights on that door, Clint snapped his gun arm up so the Colt caught the man on the chin. That dazed him just long enough for Clint to drop the Colt back into its holster, grab hold of the man's collar and belt, and then toss the man straight toward the closing door.

The man didn't exactly fly through the air, but he did stumble right where Clint wanted him to go and slammed headfirst into the door just as it was about to shut. The door flew open and knocked Dench back in the process, allowing Clint to step inside.

"All right now," Clint said as he met the killer's eyes. "Looks like it's just you and me."

FORTY-ONE

The man who was lying in the doorway started to get up, but couldn't quite manage it after getting knocked in the head by the heavy slab of wood. Instead, he laid back down and decided to fulfill his role as a doorstop.

Dench's hand flicked toward his belt and was suddenly gripping his knife. The move was so fast that Clint wondered if he would have survived if Dench's weapon of choice had been a gun.

"You're a persistent cuss, ain't you?" Dench asked.

Clint circled along with him, making sure to stay in front of Dench at all times. "Yeah. I tend to get a little bent out of shape when someone tries to gut me."

"Well, then you ain't gonna like this too much." As that last word was still hanging in the air, Dench lunged forward and swiped at Clint's stomach.

Reacting at the first hint of movement from Dench's blade, Clint stepped and leaned back a little more to clear a path for the knife. He could feel something brush along his abdomen, but the blade didn't even get close enough to shred Clint's shirt.

Dench backed off a few steps and began circling in the opposite direction. Hunkering down low, he held his knife

163

in front of him like a scorpion getting ready to sink its stinger into its prey. "I'll be a rich man after delivering your head on a platter," he said.

"Only if you think you can swing that blade faster than I can fire this gun."

"Now that ain't very sporting. What's the matter? You know I got you beat?"

Clint shook his head at the prodding words. "I'm not falling for that. You either put down that knife or I will shoot you."

"You're gonna have to shoot an unarmed man, because I'm not about to let you put your hands on me. I can already see in your eyes that you ain't the sort to shoot an unarmed man."

There was no way for Clint to deny that. Those two gunmen in the hallway had been able to read that much in the space of a second or two. Besides, Dench was still moving and circling like a snake, and putting him down with one shot wasn't exactly a safe bet.

It was a much safer bet that Dench would throw that knife into Clint's chest the moment Clint pulled his trigger.

"You talk awfully tough for a man who knows he's got an advantage so long as he's carrying a blade," Clint said. "The truth is that you know damn well you're nothing without it."

"I could take you apart with my bare hands, mate," Dench snarled as even more of his native accent leaked out.

Putting a disgusted edge into his voice, Clint replied, "I doubt that very much, little man."

Hearing those last two words was enough to bring Dench to the edge of his patience. "Toss your gun and say that again."

Clint could feel he was gaining ground. He'd pushed the right button, and now Dench was so angry that he'd become predictable. Taking another gamble, Clint threw his Colt away and said, "Come and get it, runt."

Dench's eyes flared open and a guttural snarl came from his mouth. He charged at Clint with the knife in his hand, but was too angry to put any finesse on his attack. Clint blocked it easily and pounded his fist on Dench's wrist. His knuckles drove straight into the soft spot beneath Dench's thumb and forced him to let the knife slip from his grasp.

Too angry to notice his knife was gone, Dench slammed a fist into Clint's side and then viciously snapped his head forward to catch Clint over his right eye. Although Clint could brace himself for the first punch, the head butt caught him off guard. He felt the solid impact and staggered back while fighting to keep his footing.

Judging by the unsteadiness in his own movements, Dench was also feeling some of the effects from that head butt. He staggered forward a step, shook the cobwebs from his head and then charged toward Clint with a crazed look in his eyes.

Clint jumped to one side and reached out to steady himself against the wall. Instead of the wall, however, he felt heat searing through his fingers. Clint yanked his hand back and turned to find the furnace uncomfortably close to where he was standing. He also caught sight of a young woman hogtied in the corner closest to the furnace.

The woman looked to be in her late teens or early twenties. She was also petrified to move a muscle since she was a hair's breadth away from allowing her head to touch the hot surface of the furnace.

Clint saw all of this in a matter of seconds. When he wheeled around to face Dench, he saw the smaller man reach for his boot and come up with a slender knife gripped in a tight fist.

Dench might have muttered something under his breath, but Clint was too close to the chugging furnace to hear it. He didn't need to hear a thing, however, to know what Dench's intentions were. Clint could still see the murderous look in his eyes, as well as the tensing of Dench's muscles under his skin.

After pulling in a quick breath, Dench lunged forward. He led with his knife like it was the tip of a spear, and the rest of his body provided the momentum behind it. The only way for Clint to defend against it was to give Dench the benefit of the doubt, assume the Englishman was faster than him and react in what should have been a split second too soon.

Clint twisted himself to one side and brought both arms down in a strong sweeping motion. His hands caught Dench on the back and shoulder, allowing Clint to deflect the incoming attack while forcing Dench into the hot metal of the furnace.

Dench's knife caught in the door used to shovel coal into the furnace and opened the square portal. His arms were skinny enough to make it into the little opening, and he sank his hands into the fire within. With Clint still pushing him, Dench slammed his forehead against the furnace and then bounced straight back as his entire body reacted to the heat and searing pain that followed.

Even after he'd pulled his arms from the furnace, Dench screamed like an animal. The knife was still in his hand. In fact, his skin might have melted around it.

Clint wasn't behind Dench any longer. He'd already picked up his Colt and had it ready to fire when Dench charged at him one more time. Clint pulled his trigger and sent a bullet through Dench's head. The Englishman kept coming, so Clint fired again. The second round caught Dench in the chest and knocked him to the floor like a kick from a mule.

Standing over him, Clint sighted along the top of his Colt as if he still expected Dench to get up. Although Dench let out a few last gasps, he wasn't moving anywhere.

Clint looked to the woman tied up in the corner and holstered his pistol so he could get her out of those ropes.

"You all right, ma'am?" Clint asked once he took the bandanna from over her mouth.

She seemed even younger now and was too scared to talk. Instead, she wrapped her arms around Clint and sobbed into his shirt.

When he heard someone push open the door, Clint drew his Colt and took aim in the blink of an eye.

Mia stood her ground and looked at Dench as well as the unconscious man at her feet. "Looks like I missed all the fun," she said.

"There's still some fun to be had," Clint replied. "We still need to get one of these boys to tell us where Solomon's at."

"Not enough time for that. We need to find him before he gets wind of what happened down here."

Clint looked past Mia and down the hall. Already, there were people poking their heads out to get a look.

FORTY-TWO

As Clint escorted Mia to the main poker room, nobody would have thought they'd just gotten finished fighting for their lives in the bowels of the boat. Clint was in a fresh set of clothes, and Mia was smiling as she walked arm in arm with him.

"What's so funny?" Clint asked.

"I'm not genuinely impressed by a lot of men, Clint Adams, but you sure managed to impress the hell out of me."

"What'd I do now?"

"How did you get on such good terms with that laundry lady?"

Clint looked at her and asked, "That's what impressed you?"

Mia nodded.

"We both could have been killed, but we managed to take out that last batch of Solomon's men. We even saved another hostage that we didn't even know about. After all of that, you're impressed that I was on good terms with the laundry lady?"

Mia nodded again. "What was her name?"

"Lucy," Clint said as he shifted his eyes forward so he

could open the door leading in from the deck. "Most folks call her Lucy."

Instead of stepping through the door, Mia placed her hands on Clint's cheeks and gave him a gentle kiss.

"What was that for?" Clint asked.

"That was just because you act like you don't deserve it. Besides, if you hadn't known Lucy so well, one of those workers might have run off and let the news leak to Solomon about our little scuffle in the furnace room."

"Those workers looked too scared to do much of anything. From the looks of it, I think they were just as glad to see those men get taken out of the way as we were."

"Still," Mia continued, "knowing Lucy came in pretty handy. We're actually a pretty good team. You ever think of joining the Texas Rangers?"

"I thought you said you weren't exactly a Ranger," Clint pointed out.

Mia shrugged. "I'm not, but I bet they'd let me in if I brought you along in the bargain."

"I know you hate to hear this, but I don't think you'd be as useful if they put one of those big white hats on you. You're like a shark swimming just under the water. Nobody knows you're there until you've already sunk your teeth into their leg."

"That's a nice way of saying those Texas boys would never let a woman in with the real Rangers, but I'll still take it."

Clint pulled in a breath and looked toward the main room, which was just inside the door where they were now standing. "Lucy may be able to keep those people who saw our fight quiet for a while, but I don't want to push it. Let's get this ball rolling before it's too late."

"We still don't know exactly what to look for," Mia said. "I've pieced together a few descriptions of Solomon here and there, but they could match just about any somewhat handsome man with dark hair."

"The one thing we do know is that Solomon is out to steal as much money as he can before leaving this boat with his prisoners," Clint pointed out. "He's probably already robbed a few bankrolls, but there's not much we can do about that. The best way for him to steal now is to win at a game."

"That also gives him plenty of witnesses to say he was somewhere else when those prisoners were taken or that money was stolen," Mia added.

"Good thinking. Since I managed to get a look at the cards he marked, all we should do is go in and try to find the game that's got the potential to create the biggest pots."

Mia let out a haggard sigh. "I have no idea how the hell we can find out something like that."

Clint was about to admit the same thing when he saw a potential savior walk toward the door. He smiled at the man with the salt-and-pepper hair as the door was opened for them. "Hello, Arvin," Clint said.

"Good evening, sir."

"Do you have any idea where we could find a Mr. Solomon?"

Arvin didn't even pause before answering, "I don't believe I know a Mr. Solomon."

"What about the man who stays in room number five?"

"I believe he's sitting at a table in the aft poker room."

"Are you sure?" Mia asked.

Arvin nodded. "I just delivered some refreshments to that table and they were charged to that cabin. I've seen that man walking into that room myself, otherwise I wouldn't have allowed the charge."

"Which one is he?" Clint asked.

"He has dark hair and was sitting with his back to the wall. If you'd like, I could point him out to you."

Clint reached into his pocket and placed a few folded bills into his hand. He then placed those bills into Arvin's hand as he shook it. "You've been a big help, Arvin. Thank you kindly."

When he got a look at how much money was in his hand, Arvin actually smiled. "My pleasure, sir." After that, he held the door open for Clint and Mia to enter.

They walked straight through the main room, greeted a few familiar faces and walked out the door leading to the room at the back of the boat. Once inside, they were fighting for space since the cramped quarters were packed with gamblers. Just looking at the tabletops told Clint one thing.

"This is where the money is," he whispered to Mia.

She nodded toward a table at the back of the room. "And that's where Solomon is."

Unfortunately, all but one of the men sitting there matched the rough description Arvin had given them. Also, the table was in a corner, so nearly everyone had his back to a wall.

"Nothing's ever easy," Clint said as he walked over to the table.

FORTY-THREE

Clint worked his way through the crowded room and stepped up to the table in the back corner. One of the men sitting there was raking in the pot, so Clint took the opportunity to lean in and tip his hat.

"Looks like a good game," Clint said. "Mind if I sit in?"

A few of the players recognized Clint's face and shrugged, since they didn't know him quite well enough to vouch for him directly. One of the older players stared at Clint as if he'd dropped his pants and asked the rest of the table what they thought of the sight.

"We got a full game," the older man grunted.

Another of the players shrugged and looked away from Clint as if he'd already forgotten he was there.

As the deck was being shuffled, but before a single card could be dealt, Clint sighed and reached into his jacket. "There's not a lot of seats left on this boat," Clint said as he set a stack of money onto the table with his hand firmly on top of it. "You sure you couldn't see your way clear to making some room?"

A few of the players looked around at one another, but they all seemed to be in agreement.

"Have a seat," the older spokesman said. "No reason to

keep a man out when he just wants to have a friendly game."

Clint smiled and pulled a chair over to the table. "My thoughts, exactly," he said.

The moment he sat down, a young man wearing the uniform of the boat's crew came over and changed Clint's money into chips. Drinks were brought over and the game was under way.

"My name's Clint, by the way."

The man to Clint's left nodded and said, "That'd make me Kenneth."

The older man who'd done most of the talking grumbled and shuffled the cards. Apart from a few streaks of gray in his hair, he came close to fitting the description Clint had heard regarding Solomon. Then again, so did everyone but Kenneth. Kenneth was a slender man with light blond hair. The man sitting directly across from Clint had a heavier build. The man to Clint's right was slightly skinnier than what Clint had expected. Rather than try to figure anything out, Clint sat back and played some cards.

The first hand he was dealt was a pair of threes. Since triple threes had seemed to be Clint's lucky hand on the *Misty Morning*, he pitched the other three cards and hoped for the best.

Kenneth pitched the same amount of cards after calling the small wager that had been put out by the fellow to Clint's right.

Sure enough, when his replacement cards were dealt, Clint not only got his third three, but a pair of sevens to boot. After another little bet was placed, Clint raised it by another twenty-five dollars.

"I'm out," Kenneth said as he threw his cards toward the dealer.

"Me, too," the man next to Kenneth said.

The older man rubbed his chin and nodded to himself. "I'll see that bet . . . and double it."

Although he'd been considering it before, the skinny fellow to Clint's right let out a whistle and set his cards down. "Too much for me. You two have at it."

Clint pulled in a deep breath and thought about something else as he tried to look agonized over his decision. What he truly concentrated on was the backs of the cards on the table. After studying them for a few more seconds, Clint was convinced that none of those cards were marked in the way that he'd seen in room number five.

Just to make certain the game remained interesting, Clint rattled some more chips in his hands and looked over to the only man remaining in the game. "You trying to muscle me out of this hand?" Clint asked.

"One way to find out," the man replied good-naturedly.

Clint thought his chances were pretty good of taking an even bigger chunk out of the other man's chips. Then again, it was only the first hand, and Clint had no way of knowing whether or not the man was bluffing or if he'd gotten even luckier on the draw than Clint had.

"Raise another fifty," Clint said reluctantly.

Without hesitation, the man called the bet. He moved in the chips and showed three kings with an ace and ten to back it up. "Three wise men," he said. "What've you got?"

Clint showed his full house and raked in the chips.

The older man shook his head and laughed. "You got awfully damn lucky on the draw, my friend, but that luck doesn't last."

"For my sake, I hope it does," Clint replied with a grin.

"This should prove to be an interesting game."

"I'm counting on it."

FORTY-FOUR

The game wore on for hours. Truth be told, it was one of the more interesting games Clint had played in a while. Even though he wasn't just there to play poker, Clint found himself savoring every moment. The stakes rose steadily. All the players had their moments of glory, and not one of them was prone to foolish mistakes. It was exactly the sort of thing Clint had been hoping for when he'd first opened the finely engraved invitation.

Even though that invitation had come only through a bit of trickery on behalf of the Texas Rangers, Clint was glad to be there all the same. He'd won his fair share of the pots, and the fact that the other gamblers weren't too interested in talking and swapping stories only allowed Clint to concentrate on what he was doing.

Kenneth grinned as he lay down his cards. "Flush," he announced proudly. "Queen high."

Clint and most of the other men tossed their cards amid a few muttered curses. The man across from Clint, however, looked back and forth between his cards and the ones spread out in front of Kenneth.

This man was the heavyset one with the strong features

and thick black hair that made him look more like the captain of the boat than one of its passengers. "It seems to be your night, Kenneth," the man said.

"Just playing the cards I'm dealt."

While shuffling and preparing to deal, the man across from Clint nodded and replied, "We'll just have to see what we can do about that."

Clint watched the shuffle and the deal as closely as he'd been watching all the others. He didn't see the other man make a switch or even move the cards to somewhere they were out of sight. Even so, somewhere along the line, the switch was made.

By the time Clint received his third card, he noticed something familiar. The pattern on the back of his cards was slightly altered in a way that could have easily been mistaken for normal wear and tear due to sweaty hands or careless shuffles. The irregularities weren't consistent, but Clint knew they were the same as the ones he'd seen on those cards in room number five.

Clint was dealt the ace of spades and two other spades to match. He also got two of his three lucky threes, so he kept those and the ace and discarded the rest.

The betting started off small and Clint kept it that way. When he didn't get anything to match his threes or ace, Clint was glad he hadn't been superstitious. Keeping his eyes on the man across from him, Clint called the bet that was made and watched for a move to be made.

The skinny fellow on Clint's right won the hand with a pair of sevens, and nothing else of interest came to pass. As the next several hands were played, Clint noticed the man across from him taking fewer and fewer losses. In fact, he'd even started to build up a healthy stack of chips that had been taken directly from Kenneth's pile. Those marked cards stayed in play, and Clint managed to learn a few of those markings for himself.

It wasn't until an hour later that some of the right cards fell into the right set of hands.

Clint didn't even look at his cards before he called the bet of a hundred dollars posed by the older man at the table. When the bet was raised again, Clint looked at the man who'd tossed in the additional chips and asked, "Did you hear about what happened earlier?"

"No," Kenneth replied. "What?"

"Some men were killed because they were caught cheating."

The older man nodded and the skinny fellow shrugged.

"What do you think about that, Solomon?"

Although the man across from Clint didn't say anything outright, the speed with which his eyes jumped up to look at Clint spoke volumes.

"I heard they were friends of yours," Clint said.

"Are you speaking to me?" Solomon asked.

"You know damn well I am," Clint replied. "I just thought you'd like to know that all those people you held hostage are free and all the money you stole has been accounted for."

The older man sitting next to Solomon cleared his throat and asked, "What's the meaning of all this talk?"

"I'm sure I don't know," Solomon said evenly. "Perhaps you should ask him."

Clint turned and saw Mia standing near the door. Elsa was beside her and so was Marty. Both of them talked excitedly to Mia and pointed toward Clint's table. When Mia walked up to stand behind Clint, she leaned to his ear and whispered, "Both of them say they saw that man when they were captured, but they don't know for certain it's Solomon."

"It's Solomon, all right," Clint said.

Solomon grinned and said, "Prove it."

"All right." Looking down at Solomon's cards, he said,

"I saw you swap out the deck we were using with one that you'd marked."

Although the other gamblers didn't know what to make of what Clint had been saying so far, that sure caught their attention.

"What?" Kenneth snapped.

Solomon shook his head. "He's lying. If anything, he's the one that swapped those cards."

"Don't you think I'd be sitting on top of more chips if that was the case?" Clint asked.

The other gamblers looked at Clint's stack, which was less than half the size it had been at the start. Solomon's, on the other hand, had nearly tripled.

"And you got most of those chips fairly recently," Clint said. He then looked around to the rest of the men at the table and announced, "This man's wanted for kidnapping and cheating. If any of you men were afraid to talk before, you should know that the gunmen Solomon brought with him are either dead or being held until we get back to a safe dock."

When no response came, Solomon grinned and said, "Nice try. Unfortunately, that was a bluff you didn't want to try." With that, Solomon snapped his fingers and waited for someone to carry out his order.

Nobody came.

As Solomon's smile faded, the skinny man next to Clint lifted his hand to show the pistol he held. "I was to hand this over when the time came," he said to Clint as he handed the gun to him. "Take it."

Clint took the gun as Solomon grabbed the edge of the table with both hands. "You're dead!"

"He's right, Mr. Solomon," the skinny man said. "None of the men are anywhere to be seen. They were supposed to come in here and take all the money from—"

"Shut up!" Solomon snapped.

Turning to Clint, the skinny man explained, "They were

supposed to have robbed everyone in this room by now. He wanted me to work for him because lots of these men trust me. He said if I didn't, he'd kill my wife."

"What's your wife look like?" Clint asked.

In a rushed flow of words, the skinny man described the young woman that Clint had found tied up in the furnace room.

"She's fine," Clint said. "You can see her shortly."

"Are you joking?"

"No, I—"

"What the hell's all this about cheating?" Kenneth snarled. "I want my goddamn money back!"

"You won't get nothing back," Solomon replied sternly. "I'm not a cheat."

"The cards are marked," Clint said. "He's holding the ace of hearts, the queen of diamonds and the queen of spades. I don't know what the other two are."

Kenneth reached across the table and flipped over Solomon's cards. Those three cards were there, just as Clint had promised. "Son of a bitch," Kenneth muttered.

Just then, Solomon stood up and drew a pistol that had been tucked under his belt. He aimed it at Clint and thumbed the hammer back before another shot blasted through the room.

Clint had jumped to his feet, but didn't have a gun in his hand. Kenneth, on the other hand, was holding a derringer that he'd stashed up his coat sleeve.

"Nobody cheats me, you son of a bitch!" Kenneth said. "Nobody!"

Solomon slumped into his chair. His eyes were still fixed on Clint, but his body was quickly losing the strength to follow through with anything but a pained wheeze. As more blood pumped from the fresh wound in his chest, Solomon let out one last breath and dropped his pistol.

Everyone in the room was watching what happened.

One of the gamblers asked, "Was that another goddamn cheater?"

"Yes," Clint replied. "He was."

"Serves him right then. Dump him in the water and deal the next hand."

FORTY-FIVE

Clint returned to Labyrinth a little later than expected, since he'd had to explain some things to a group of Texas Rangers as the rest of Solomon's men were taken off the *Misty Morning*. Mia, Elsa and Gretchen said their good-byes, and Clint soon found himself in Rick's Place telling Hartman about the affair.

Rick leaned on the bar, nodding every so often and occasionally drinking from a mug of beer. When Clint was finished, Rick still didn't say much of anything.

"I swear," Clint said as he picked up his own beer, "I can't go anywhere without it going to hell."

"You didn't even get any gambling done?"

"Actually, I did. I even turned a nice little profit."

"What about our arrangement?" Rick asked. "Did you manage to spread the word about this place to earn the money I put toward your bankroll?"

Clint stared at Hartman over the top of his mug. Since the Texan knew him too well to believe a bluff, Clint put his mug down and dug into the pocket where he kept his winnings. "Serves me right for doing a good deed," Clint muttered.

Rick laughed, but didn't lift a finger to stop Clint from peeling off the right number of bills from the hefty roll of cash.

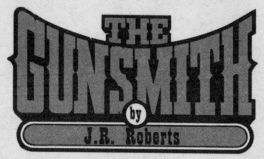